THE OFFICE GRAPEVINE

Barrington Corporation News Bulletin
Vol.1 No. 1
January 1999

• Everyone's talking about Cindy Cooper's great makeover. Who knew that girl was just a swan waiting to happen? And the looks her boss is giving her…. Do we hear wedding bells? Finally?

• Big news, indeed, for all you single gals. Rex Barrington III is coming to town. Well, rumor has it that he's taking over the business for his father. And the billionaire needs a new assistant. Which one of our lucky gals will be this executive's right-hand woman?

• And who can tell us why that Olivia McGovern was turning positively green at lunch last week? Could she be… expecting? And who in the world—or in the office—could be that baby's daddy?

Dear Reader,

Silhouette Romance is proud to usher in the year with *two* exciting new promotions! LOVING THE BOSS is a six-book series, launching this month and ending in June, about office romances leading to happily-ever-afters. In the premiere title, *The Boss and the Beauty*, by award-winning author Donna Clayton, a prim personal assistant wows her jaded, workaholic boss when she has a Cinderella makeover....

You've asked for more family-centered stories, so we created FAMILY MATTERS, an ongoing promotion with a special flash. The launch title, *Family by the Bunch* from popular Special Edition author Amy Frazier, pairs a rancher in want of a family with a spirited social worker...and *five* adorable orphans.

Also available are more of the authors you love, and the miniseries you've come to cherish. Kia Cochrane's emotional Romance debut, *A Rugged Ranchin' Dad*, beautifully captures the essence of FABULOUS FATHERS. Star author Judy Christenberry unveils her sibling-connected miniseries LUCKY CHARM SISTERS with *Marry Me, Kate*, an unforgettable marriage-of-convenience tale. *Granted: A Family for Baby* is the latest of Carol Grace's BEST-KEPT WISHES miniseries. And COWBOYS TO THE RESCUE, the heartwarming Western saga by rising star Martha Shields, continues with *The Million-Dollar Cowboy*.

Enjoy this month's offerings, and look forward to more spectacular stories coming each month from Silhouette Romance!

Happy New Year!

Mary-Theresa Hussey

Mary-Theresa Hussey
Senior Editor, Silhouette Romance

Please address questions and book requests to:
Silhouette Reader Service
U.S.: 3010 Walden Ave., P.O. Box 1325, Buffalo, NY 14269
Canadian: P.O. Box 609, Fort Erie, Ont. L2A 5X3

THE BOSS AND THE BEAUTY

Donna Clayton

Silhouette

R O M A N C E™

Published by Silhouette Books

America's Publisher of Contemporary Romance

Silhouette Romance would like to thank Donna Fasano,
writing as Donna Clayton, for her contribution to the
Loving the Boss series.

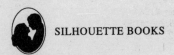 SILHOUETTE BOOKS

SISBN 0-373-19342-4

THE BOSS AND THE BEAUTY

Copyright © 1999 by Harlequin Books S.A.

Printed in U.S.A.

Books by Donna Clayton

Silhouette Romance

Mountain Laurel #720
Taking Love in Stride #781
Return of the Runaway Bride #999
Wife for a While #1039
Nanny and the Professor #1066
Fortune's Bride #1118
Daddy Down the Aisle #1162
*Miss Maxwell Becomes a Mom #1211
*Nanny in the Nick of Time #1217
*Beauty and the Bachelor Dad #1223
†The Stand-By Significant Other #1284
†Who's the Father of Jenny's Baby? #1302
The Boss and the Beauty #1342

*The Single Daddy Club
†Mother & Child

DONNA CLAYTON

is proud to be a recipient of the Holt Medallion, an award honoring outstanding literary talent for her Silhouette Romance novel, *Wife for a While*. And seeing her work appear on the Waldenbooks Series Bestsellers List has given her a great deal of joy and satisfaction.

Reading is one of Donna's favorite ways to while away a rainy afternoon. She loves to hike, too. Another hobby added to her list of fun things to do is traveling. She fell in love with Europe during her first trip abroad recently, and plans to return often. Oh, and Donna still collects cookbooks, but as her writing career grows, she finds herself using them less and less.

Donna loves to hear from her readers. Please write to her in care of Silhouette Books, 300 East 42nd Street, New York, NY 10017.

Dear Reader,

Silhouette Romance is very excited about our first in-line continuity series, LOVING THE BOSS, beginning in January 1999, to be followed by one new title each month for the next five months. This brand-new six-book series about office romances that lead to happily-ever-after features sexy, powerful heroes and lovely, feisty heroines. In LOVING THE BOSS, you'll meet six friends who work for the same company and who all dream of marrying their respective bosses. Each month, one of these heroines will find love with the man of her dreams—who may, or may not, be her boss!

We are thrilled with the terrific lineup of authors and stories we have for our readers. Each LOVING THE BOSS title has been written by one of your favorite Silhouette Romance writers. The titles in this series are:

These six heartwarming stories are not to be missed. Be sure to look for these LOVING THE BOSS titles in your local bookstores. Enjoy!

The Editors of Silhouette Books

Prologue

The seconds were ticking down. Cindy Cooper sneaked a quick peek at her wristwatch.

Eight minutes before midnight. Eight minutes before the party being held downstairs in the Barrington Corporation auditorium would erupt with shouts of "Happy New Year!" Eight short minutes before resolutions were revealed and good wishes were exchanged along with a few hugs and kisses....

That thought forced Cindy's gaze to ever so slowly lift over the rim of her eyeglasses and surreptitiously focus on the man sitting behind the huge, oak desk across the room. His head was bent as he studied the files on his desktop. The lamplight glistened against the thick waves of his mahogany hair, and his broad, suit-clad shoulders were slightly rounded in his preoccupation with the project plans. The fingers that flipped through the pages of text were bronzed and strong, as were his hands. And his forearms.

Oh, his arms might be covered by a black suit jacket tonight because of the office party going on downstairs—a party they had slipped away from to go over a few details of the project—but Cindy had seen him often enough in his shirtsleeves, his cuffs rolled up to his elbows, as they had worked many an evening long after normal business hours. All she had to do to conjure a vivid image of his olive skin, his corded muscles, was close her eyes.

Kyle Prentice. The man who occupied her fantasies. The man who had stolen her heart and didn't even know he held the prize in his possession. The vice president of the New Products division. The man for whom she acted as personal assistant.

In the plainest words, *Cindy Cooper was desperately attracted to her boss.* And he didn't have a clue how she felt.

Dipping her head, Cindy tried to concentrate on the prospectus sheets balanced on her lap. But the neat lines of figures blurred together, and all Cindy could think about was the lively music being played four floors below—and the missed opportunities to dance in Kyle's arms. Not that he had much interest in dancing with her, but he *might* have asked her a time or two, if they were downstairs with the others rather than up here all alone.

Soon the magical hour would strike, and champagne corks would pop. Fun and laughter were being enjoyed by all the Barrington Corp. employees and their party guests.

All of them, that was, except her. And Kyle. Again her eyes darted to him.

Oh, why did he have to be so intensely focused or

work? she lamented. Why was he so conscientious? And why, for goodness' sake, did he have to be so darned attractive?

Cindy paused, shifting her weight on the smooth leather couch. But weren't those the very reasons that her feelings for Kyle ran so deep? His intensity regarding, his passion for, his utter devotion to what he did for a living. Not to mention his to-die-for chocolate brown eyes. If she could only capture—*really* capture—his attention, even for just a moment or two....

A forlorn sigh threatened to escape her lips, but Cindy expertly contained it as she wondered why on earth Kyle would ever notice her. With her plain brown hair and her average green eyes, she knew she was no great beauty. Hadn't she been told that all through her childhood?

But she was dedicated to Kyle, to the New Projects division and to Barrington Corp., working seemingly endless overtime hours, never complaining—in fact, always quite eager—when her boss asked her to stay at the office. Surely those things were important. Surely her commitment and loyalty were enough to attract Kyle's attention.

Three quick raps on the office door had both her and Kyle lifting their heads. Mildred Van Hess, the longtime personal assistant to company president, Rex Barrington II, poked her head around the door.

"I can't believe you two are working," she told them. Then she sighed, her eyes twinkling fondly. "Well, on second thought, maybe I can."

Kyle smiled, one corner of his mouth curling in that sexy manner that never failed to cause Cindy's pulse to thump erratically. If only that smile was leveled on her rather than on Mildred. Ah, well, she could dream, couldn't she?

"Cindy and I decided to come up and go over a few details of the new project," he told Mildred. "You know we'll be giving the presentation to Mr. Barrington in two short weeks."

"Yes, and we're all excited about the unveiling," Mildred said. "We can't wait to find out what you two have come up with. But the New Year will be ringing in in just minutes, and you two need to come downstairs and rejoin the party. That's a direct order from none other than the head honcho himself." The woman's tone lowered to a conspiratorial level as she added, "He plans to make a big announcement just after midnight."

"Oh?" Kyle's brows rose with curiosity.

Then Mildred focused her attention on Cindy.

"Do you think you can talk this man into coming back to the party?"

Cindy's heart hammered with excitement. She could just hug Mildred. There was nothing she wanted more than to put away the files and join the others.

Reaching up and pulling her eyeglasses off her face, Cindy said, "I'll do what I can." She'd placed just the right amount of feigned seriousness in her tone to make the older woman chuckle.

"Good," Mildred said. "Mr. Barrington wants this to be the perfect New Year's Eve for everybody."

The door latch gave a soft click as Mildred left the office, and Cindy looked at Kyle.

"Just give me another minute or two," Kyle told her. "And then we'll go on down."

"Sure." Cindy nodded, feeling a twinge of frustration that they weren't going to just pick up and rejoin the party immediately.

A couple of minutes. Certainly she could wait that long. She could spend the time pondering exactly what would constitute the perfect New Year's Eve that Mildred had mentioned.

For Kyle, Cindy knew, the components were simple: long overtime hours spent buried under a mountain of work. One corner of her mouth curled ironically. The man must be in heaven right about now.

However, for herself, she knew the night would have to be very different if it were to be described as perfect.

Soft music and candlelight, a bottle or two of Chardonnay, a slow, sexy dance while pressed tightly against the man of her dreams. She could almost hear the music, feel the hard mass of Kyle's chest under her palms, as the vision took on a strange, nearly corporal quality.

Five seconds before midnight, his fingers slid, gently caressing, along her jaw. He tipped up her chin until their gazes locked. The fierce hunger expressed in his deep brown eyes made her blood heat, her heart thump.

"You're my whole world," he whispered. "My whole life."

Overwhelming desire had his tone low and rough, and shivers coursed across every inch of her skin.

And then he captured her lips with his. She was aware of a dozen sensations at once. His mouth was

hot and moist against hers, his tongue ardently de-
manding, and Cindy was most willing to surrender.

His kiss ushered in the New Year in a manner that
made her knees go weak. She hung on to his broad
shoulders for dear life, yet her soul sang with pure
joy.

Cindy started with a tiny jerk. What a dream she
had conjured! What a night she'd imagined! Oh, if
only...

Her eyes widened when she remembered the time,
and she glanced at her watch. Five seconds before
midnight. Four. Three. Two. One.

Well, the New Year had arrived. And it had come
with no bells and whistles. No confetti or champagne.
No resolutions or good wishes. Not a hug...nor even
one passionate kiss.

Disappointment knotted painfully in her throat. But
she wouldn't let her frustration show. She wouldn't
allow her deep longing to surface. Not when she had
to go face her friends and co-workers down in the
auditorium. Not when everyone was trying to have a
good time at the party. She refused to dampen their
merriment and good spirits. And she'd be darned if
she'd allow Kyle to see that she was upset.

No, she'd lift her head high. She'd smile her bright-
est smile, laugh her gayest laugh. She'd make sure
that no one saw her pain, that no one knew she was
hurting.

Feeling utterly miserable, Cindy clamped her bottom lip between her teeth and silently wished herself
a happy New Year.

Chapter One

Cindy slid shut the filing cabinet drawer and then moved to her desk to tidy it before leaving the office for the day. She worked quickly, hoping that Kyle wouldn't stop in and ask her to work overtime this evening. Any other time she'd have been happy to stay. But she had plans this evening. Important plans. At least they were to her.

Irritation pricked at her like a barbed saguaro—irritation directed at Kyle. But as soon as she realized its presence, Cindy did her best to at least ignore it since she found it impossible to make it go away.

In the week and a half since the New Year's Eve party, Cindy found herself feeling…strange. Emotions would rise up in her at odd moments: annoyance, discontent, bitterness, hurt. So far, she'd been able to hide these things from her boss and her co-workers. So far, her job performance hadn't been affected. But the overwhelming feelings were getting the best of her. Especially today.

Oh, she knew perfectly well why her emotions were becoming more than she could handle. Stress was the cause. Stress and disappointment in dealing with her attraction for Kyle—an attraction that continued to go unnoticed by him. She was going to have to do something. She certainly wouldn't allow her feelings to get in the way of her doing her job. She'd mastered the runaway emotions up to now. But she'd had a devil of a time wrestling with them today.

If only he'd remembered her special day....

The quick raps on her open office door had her chin lifting. Normally, she had a welcome smile ready for Kyle whenever he appeared in her office or she met him in the hallway. But for the life of her, she just couldn't summon one now.

He carried a huge black binder in his arms and several files. "You're not leaving, are you?" he asked. "I have a few documents to look over, and one more call to make, but I was hoping—"

"I can't stay." She cut him off before he could make the request for her to work late. After taking a second to control herself, she quietly explained, "I have plans."

"Oh. Well, in that case..."

He seemed taken by surprise. Guilt sliced through her like a knife. She was a conscientious employee, and she hated disappointing her boss. Normally, working late with Kyle was more than simply a job, it was pretty much a selfish thing. She loved being in his company. Loved getting caught up in the work.

Loved getting lost in his intense enthusiasm for the projects they made happen. However, this evening was different.

"I'm having dinner," Cindy told him. "With friends."

His gorgeous, dark eyes lit with a thought.

"You're having a night out with the girls."

She nodded. Irritation flared again. She'd be darned if she told him the real reason behind the dinner…the fact that there was a celebration afoot. *Her* celebration!

And why, when she said she was going out with friends, did he automatically assume she would be with "the girls"? Why, she just might be going out with a rowdy group of randy males.

Well, a small, sane voice silently spoke up in her mind, *that really is impossible seeing as how your work in the New Products division keeps you too busy to develop friendships outside of Barrington. Besides, you're not interested in dating anyone anyway. Besides your boss, that is.*

Those facts didn't matter, she thought, realizing full well she was being stubborn, maybe even a little immature, but unable to do a thing about it at the moment. Kyle still had no right to make any assumptions regarding her social life.

"By all means," he said, "go and have a great time."

In the blink of an eye, he was gone. And Cindy was left all alone. Seething to the marrow of her bones.

"It's my birthday," she informed the empty room through gritted teeth. "And you forgot, Kyle. Again."

A full thirty seconds had passed before she got a controlling grip on her hurt and resentful feelings. She had to do something about this situation. She had to do something *drastic*.

"Happy birthday, dear Cindy," the four women sang in unison, even if their concerted effort was a little off-key, "happy birthday to you."

Having forced all the depressing feelings aside, Cindy offered her friends a huge smile. "Aw, you guys are sweet," she told them. An elaborately decorated birthday cake, its thirty candles blazing, sat in the middle of the table. "But what are you trying to do?" Teasing sarcasm thickened her tone. "Blind every resident of Phoenix with all these candles?"

Rachel Sinclair chuckled. "Well, blow them out already. The light *is* beginning to hurt my eyes."

An accountant for Barrington, Rachel was the first person Cindy had befriended when coming to work for the company.

"The candles on my cake might make a mighty blaze," Cindy quipped to Rachel, "but yours will always burn brighter than mine."

"Don't remind me," Rachel moaned. "Everyone here already knows I'm the oldest one in the group."

Cindy grinned. "And we don't intend to let you forget it, either," she teased. Then she leaned toward the cake.

"Wait!" Molly Doyle put her hand on Cindy's sleeve.

Molly worked in the advertising department. She was a creative genius when it came to promotion and marketing.

"You've got to make a wish," Molly went on. "A woman gets so few opportunities to wish for her heart's desire."

"That's the truth." Olivia McGovern, a paralegal at Barrington, reached for her glass of water, its ice cubes tinkling.

"And if I know Cindy," Sophia Shepherd said, "her wish will have something to do with one Mr. Kyle Prentice."

Cindy's gaze widened as she looked at Sophia. The usually withdrawn and quiet secretary had surprised Cindy by mentioning Kyle.

Heat suddenly suffused Cindy's face, and she pressed her fingers to her cheeks. She shouldn't feel embarrassed. These women were her friends. They knew what was happening between herself and Kyle. Or rather, what *wasn't* happening.

No, she commanded silently. *No bad feelings allowed. Not tonight. Not when I'm celebrating my birthday.* Again she leaned toward the blazing cake.

"The wish," Rachel pointedly reminded her.

"Okay, okay," Cindy said. As soon as she lowered her eyelids, images of Kyle's handsome face floated before her. For a second, she couldn't decide whether to wish for a simple kiss from the man, or to go all out and wish for a full-fledged marriage proposal. A rough chuckle erupted from her throat.

"What's so funny?" Molly asked.

Cindy simply shook her head. "Nothing," she said,

realizing the ironic truth: she could either laugh about her predicament or she could cry. Tonight she intended to laugh.

Deciding she might as well wish for the whole shebang, she silently recited her marital hopes and then blew out the candles with one big puff. Although she knew good and well it was one wasted wish.

The rest of the women cheered and clapped, and Cindy pushed her eyeglasses back into place, pulled out a chair and sat down.

"Oh," Olivia said, "I hope everyone doesn't mind. I invited Patricia."

"Peel?" Cindy said.

Sophia's brows rose a fraction. "From Personnel?"

Olivia nodded. "She's so shy. I thought it would do her good to meet us all. You know, get a chance to come out of her shell a little. Become one of the group."

There were silent nods and smiles of agreement all around.

Rachel turned to Olivia. "You wouldn't happen to know if she's over thirty-one, would you?"

"Sorry," Olivia said, lifting a sympathetic shoulder, "but I think she's younger."

"Figures," Rachel mumbled.

Cindy laughed. "You're just destined to be the oldest. Get over it."

"Patricia told me she had a meeting," Olivia said, "and that she might be a little late—" She glanced toward the door, her face brightening. "Oh, here she is now." She beckoned to Patricia with a hearty wave.

Friendly greetings were passed back and forth.

"Sorry I'm late," Patricia said to everyone at large. Then she focused on Cindy. "Happy birthday."

"Thanks," Cindy responded. "Make room, ladies. Patricia, sit, sit. I'm glad you could come."

Chair legs raked the floor as space was made for another seat.

Patricia eased herself into the chair and rested her elbows on the table. She sighed. "I feel like my whole life has become one big meeting since the year began."

"Because of Mr. Barrington's announcement?" Olivia asked.

Patricia nodded.

"Can you believe," Rachel commented, "that he declared his intention to retire at the New Year's Eve party?"

Molly's eyes rounded. "I thought I'd faint dead away when he told us."

"Maybe," Cindy piped up, "he thought announcing his retirement at the party would allow us to take the news as a kind of celebration. Maybe he wanted to keep us from worrying. I'm sure he wanted us to see this as a good thing."

"Well, he might have intended to save us all some anxiety," Sophia said, "but the whole company is still in an uproar."

"I know rumors are running rampant in the legal department," Olivia agreed.

"And poor Mildred," Rachel said. "What's going to happen to her?"

"She's been Mr. Barrington's personal assistant

since—'' Cindy searched the ceiling for just the right word ''—*forever.*''

''Do you think she'll be forced into retirement, too?''

Olivia addressed the entire group, but Cindy saw that her gaze was leveled on Patricia. As assistant personnel director, Patricia would know Mildred Van Hess's fate more so than anyone else. One by one all the women turned their attention to Patricia.

''As loyal as Mildred has been,'' Patricia said quietly, ''to Mr. Barrington *and* Barrington Corp., she won't be forced to do anything. There will be a job for her for as long as she wants to work.''

Cindy could feel the air lighten as everyone's relief became apparent.

''What *I* want to know,'' Sophia said, ''is who's going to take over for Mr. Barrington?''

Concern bit into Sophia's brow and Cindy reached out and touched her forearm. Sophia was such a worrier.

Again, everyone turned their eager and curious eyes on Patricia. From the look on Patricia's face, Cindy could tell the woman had no idea who the president's successor would be. However, it was evident her mind was churning, and Cindy could clearly see Patricia wanted to be able to tell them something. She looked so anxious and eager to fit in with the group.

''There is one possibility,'' Patricia began.

Cindy nearly grinned as all her friends grew silent and leaned closer. Heck, she followed suit. Everyone wanted to be privy to important information.

''Now, this is just a rumor,'' Patricia prefaced.

"But I've heard that it could be Mr. Barrington's son. Rex, the Third." Then she repeated, "Remember now, it's just a rumor."

"But isn't he currently in charge of the overseas division?" Rachel asked.

Patricia nodded.

"Hmm," Molly said, her eyes glinting with humor, "I wonder if he's single."

Sophia plucked a tortilla chip from the basket on the table. "*I* wonder if he's cute."

Laughter lightened the mood.

"Wouldn't it be something—" Sophia suddenly grew thoughtful "—if the Third were to arrive and fall in love with one of us. Something like that could lead to marriage."

"It would be something, all right," Rachel said.

Olivia added, "A miracle is what it would be." She reached out and slid the bowl of gooey, green guacamole dip toward Sophia. "Here," she told Sophia, "take the dip over there. I think I must be coming down with the flu because the sight of that stuff is making me a little queasy."

The moment love and marriage had been mentioned, Cindy felt disappointment creeping up on her like a stealthy shadow. The best solution, she knew, was to change the subject.

"Where's the waitress?" she asked. "I'm starved. Let's order some dinner. Then we can cut that beautiful cake."

Several minutes were spent choosing food from the menu.

After the waitress walked away, Rachel said, "So what were we talking about?"

"We were fantasizing," Sophia said. "About marrying the Third."

In spite of her discomfort with the topic, Cindy had to chuckle over the name her friend had chosen for Mr. Barrington's son. If she knew this group of ladies, and she did, the nickname would stick to the man like glue.

"Well," Molly said, "the man I marry is going to be gentle. A sensitive soul." She smiled wistfully. "A man who wants at least five kids."

Toying with the edge of her linen napkin, Cindy studied Molly. The woman never talked about her parents or siblings, only dreamed about the huge loving family she intended to have one day. There was more to Molly than met the eye.

"Stable and dependable," Olivia softly offered. "Those are traits I'm looking for."

And Stanley Whitcomb, Olivia's boss, surely fit that bill perfectly. Cindy thought that Stanley was a little too old for Olivia, but if a relationship with him would make her friend happy, then she'd be delighted.

"What about excitement?" Rachel asked. "And passion?"

"Fancy Ms. Straitlaced here," Cindy observed, "crowing about passion."

"Everyone needs a little passion," Rachel murmured. Then everyone laughed, including Rachel.

"Security is the key," Olivia finally declared.

"How about you, Patricia?" Sophia asked. "What are you looking for in a husband?"

Patricia remained silent, panic flashing in her light green eyes. The color flooding her face hinted at a mysterious tale of its own.

She's in love, Cindy mused. *Deeply in love. She's harboring a secret crush. How interesting.* Cindy couldn't help but wonder who the lucky man might be.

"Leave the woman alone," Rachel admonished. "She's new to the group. You can't expect her to spill her guts right from the start."

"Yes," Molly added firmly, "let her get to know us a bit first." She leaned forward in her seat, waggling her eyebrows. "Then we'll force her to spill her guts."

Olivia tucked a strand of her long, auburn hair behind her ear. "You haven't told us, Birthday Girl," she said to Cindy, "what did Kyle do for your birthday?"

"Yes, yes," Molly said. "Tell us everything. Did he send you flowers?"

"Or was it chocolates?" Sophia asked.

Cindy felt the definite urge to groan. It was time to fess up. These were her friends, and they didn't deserve to be lied to. Inhaling deeply, she steeled herself.

Her voice was quiet, her head shaking as she said, "He didn't do anything."

There was a moment of silence as everyone absorbed what she said, and the implications of it.

"Oh, honey," Rachel said, "I'm sorry." She reached out and touched Cindy on the wrist.

"Maybe he's planning to do something tomorrow," Patricia gently suggested.

"Yes," Sophia added, "maybe he got the date wrong."

Cindy shook her head. "No, he didn't get the date wrong. He forgot the date altogether."

"You can't be sure of that," Olivia said.

"Oh, but I am," Cindy responded. "I'm very sure. And it's time for me to face the facts. Kyle's never going to take an interest in me as a woman. As his assistant, maybe. But never as a flesh-and-blood woman." Finally she sighed. "I've come to the conclusion that…it might be time to give up on Kyle."

The admission was depressing. To all of them. When one of them lost their hope and dream of finding true love, then the dreams of all of them became a little tarnished and seemingly far out of reach.

After a moment of silent commiseration, Rachel said, "Cindy, have you ever thought of…taking a different tack?"

"What do you mean?"

"Well…" Rachel paused. "First off, I want you to remember that I'm your friend. I don't want your feelings to be hurt by what I'm about to suggest."

Curiosity knit Cindy's brow, but it didn't keep her from responding warmly, "I know you love me. Feel free to say whatever you feel needs to be said."

Resting her elbows on the table, Rachel said, "You have a lovely wardrobe. Your long, full skirts and flat-heeled shoes are…professional looking. Comfortable.

Very, um, how should I say it? Decent. But have you ever thought of changing your style? Maybe getting a little...*racy?*''

Rachel's face tinged pink, like she couldn't believe she'd actually made the suggestion.

Laughter bubbled from Molly. ''I get it! Cindy, what she's saying is that you should buy yourself a few *indecent* outfits. Some short skirts that might turn Kyle's head. You certainly have the body to pull it off.''

''That's not a bad idea,'' Sophia said. ''And I'm sure a visit to the hair salon would do wonders. Cindy would look beautiful with a little curl in her hair, don't you think?''

''A perm, maybe,'' Olivia embellished the notion. ''And those glasses hide your lovely green eyes, Cindy. Maybe a little mascara would bring them out.''

Panic churned in Cindy's stomach like the massive tornado in *The Wizard Of Oz.* No, no, no! She couldn't do as they were suggesting. She simply refused to use her physical attributes as bait to catch a man.

''You don't understand,'' Cindy told them vehemently. ''I want Kyle to notice me because I'm a good person. Because I'm competent and helpful to him. Because I'm dependable and caring. I want him notice me for *who I am,* not what I look like.''

Cindy knew they could never understand. They could never see why it was so important to her to be loved for her intelligence, her character. She could never live with the idea that Kyle was interested in her because of some silly *physical* attraction. Not after what she'd seen happen in her own home.

"Okay, okay," Rachel crooned softly, "so it was a stupid suggestion—"

"It wasn't stupid" came a reply.

"I thought it was a good idea," someone else said.

Utter distress kept Cindy from hearing exactly who said what.

"Maybe she should just think about it."

It was then that the waitress arrived with platters of hot and fragrant food, and as Cindy slowly slid her glasses up onto the bridge of her nose, she was quite aware that she'd completely lost her appetite.

Chapter Two

That Friday, Kyle arrived in the office earlier than usual. He and Cindy would be presenting their new idea to Mr. Barrington this afternoon. Kyle had just settled down with his second cup of coffee and was rereading the meeting notes he'd prepared when movement at his door caught his eye.

"Good morning, Rachel," he called, prompting the woman to enter his office.

"Good morning," she said.

Knowing Rachel was a good friend of Cindy's, Kyle said, "I don't think Cindy's arrived yet. She usually gets in right at eight-thirty." One corner of his mouth tipped up into a smile. "And she's never been late."

"Actually, I came to speak to you," Rachel said.

"Oh?" He had to admit, he was surprised. "What can I do for you?"

"You can, ah," she said, "let me borrow Cindy this morning."

"Borrow...Cindy?" Rachel had him very curious now. He set down his coffee cup.

"Y-yes, well, you see," Rachel stammered. "The girls wanted to give Cindy a gift. It was...we wanted..."

She huffed in frustration, and it was obvious to Kyle that she was trying to tell him something without revealing everything. He sat back, resting his elbow on the arm of his chair.

Then she softly blurted, "This past Wednesday was Cindy's birthday. The girls want to take her out this morning and get her hair done, buy her a new outfit. As a gift. We pitched in. We know today's a big day for her, with the presentation and all."

"Cindy had a birthday on Wednesday?"

The question slipped from his lips before he could stop it, and he knew the instant the words were spoken that he'd broken his number-one rule: avoid personal involvement of any and all kinds.

Rachel nodded. "The birth date's got to be in her personnel file. As her boss—"

"Yes," he said, cutting off the censure he heard in Rachel's tone. Rachel's use of the word *boss* felt like a quick cuff on the jaw. He was Cindy's boss. Period. Nothing more, nothing less. "I've seen her file."

But you skipped over all the personal stuff, reading only what was absolutely necessary to discern that Cindy was qualified to be your personal assistant, the words echoed through his brain. Then the silent voice reminded him, *Remember the rule against becoming personally involved. You had sound reasons for making it.*

"A little pampering would be good for Cindy," he said, hoping his easy tone made up for his gruff interruption. "Especially today. Just have her back before two. The meeting is to start promptly at two."

"Oh, don't you worry," Rachel said, an amiable, almost impish grin pulling at her mouth. "She'll be back."

After Rachel left, Kyle stared at the empty doorway for several seconds. Something in the woman's parting remark left him with a vague, unsettling feeling that trouble was brewing.

Shaking his head, he murmured, "Don't be an idiot, Prentice. All Rachel did was promise to have Cindy back in time for the meeting."

He focused his attention once again on his presentation notes. But the odd anxiety continued to hover over him, stirring up an edginess in him that he hadn't felt for a long while....

Cindy parked her car in the lot, picked up her leather satchel and started across the asphalt lot toward the double glass doors of Barrington's front entrance. Her steps slowed when she spied Rachel, Olivia and Molly pushing out the doors and coming toward her.

"Hey, guys," she said, chuckling, "it's awfully early to be *leaving* the building, don't you think?"

Cheerful greetings were exchanged, and then Cindy's gaze narrowed on Olivia's face. "Are you feeling okay?'' Cindy asked. ''You look a little pale.''

''I do believe I'm coming down with something,'' Olivia complained softly.

''Are you up to going with us?'' Concern wrinkled Molly's brow.

''Absolutely,'' Olivia said, her voice sounding stronger. ''I wouldn't miss this for the world!''

''Miss what?'' Sudden interest pumped through Cindy's body like a quick shot of caffeine. ''Where're you guys going?''

''Not 'you guys,''' Rachel said.

''*Us* guys,'' Molly added. ''*You're* going, too.''

''B-but,'' Cindy stammered. However, before she could get out a complete thought, Molly had taken her satchel from her and Rachel had spun her around until she was facing away from the building.

''I can't go anywhere,'' Cindy protested, allowing herself to be propelled a few steps. ''I have too much to do. The presentation is today. I've got to check to make sure the arrangements I made for the conference room are going smoothly. I have copies to make. I have to touch base with Catering about the coffee and Danishes.''

''Everything will be taken care of,'' Rachel assured her. ''Patricia's going to handle everything.''

''But Kyle's waiting for me,'' Cindy said, trying without success to turn her head to look at Barrington Corp. ''We planned to go over our notes together.''

Molly laughed. ''If I know you and Kyle, you've both been over that presentation three times already.''

"Well, yes," Cindy reluctantly admitted, "we have. But he's expecting me."

"No, he isn't," Olivia told her. "Rachel got Kyle's permission."

"Permission for what?" Cindy turned her gaze on Rachel.

The woman grinned. "He told me I could borrow you this morning."

"Borrow me?" Cindy grumbled. "Isn't this more like *kidnapping?*"

"Exactly." Molly's eyes glittered merrily with laughter. "Come along quietly, sweetheart—" her voice dipped low in a humorous gangster imitation "—and nobody will get hurt."

"But where are we going?"

By then they had reached Molly's sleek, white Lexus. As Cindy found herself ushered into the back seat by Rachel, she couldn't help but wonder for the umpteenth time how Molly managed to afford such a car. However, the thought flitted away as she said, "Guys, today really isn't a good day for...for whatever it is you have planned. I have work to do."

"We'll have you back in plenty of time."

Rachel's pat on the hand was meant as some sort of reassurance, Cindy was sure. But Cindy wasn't reassured.

"Can you at least tell me where we're going?" she asked.

"You'll find out soon enough," Olivia said, getting into the front with Molly. The sly smile she tossed over her shoulder hinted at something very exciting.

With a frustrated sigh, Cindy latched her seat belt,

sat back against the smooth leather seat and awaited her fate.

They traveled toward the very center of Phoenix. Molly expertly maneuvered through the morning traffic, and before Cindy was put through too much miserable waiting and wondering, the car was parked, the engine cut off.

"Okay," Molly sang, "everybody out."

The three of them hustled Cindy along one block and then approached what looked like a newly renovated building.

When she saw the sign in the window, Cindy dug in her heels. "Wait just a minute," she said.

"Oh, now," Rachel said. "Be a sport, Cindy."

"We all chipped in," Molly said. "This is a belated birthday present."

Olivia nudged Cindy forward. "Let us do something nice for you. Please."

"We've set you up for the works," Rachel said. "Massage, facial, makeup, hairstyling, manicure. Heck, the shop threw in a pedicure for free."

Cindy's gaze left the Body Beauty Spa window and then briefly lighted on each of her friends' faces. They looked so excited, so pleased with themselves for offering her this gift. How could she refuse? To turn them down would surely hurt their feelings.

With her shoulders rounding in surrender, Cindy allowed them to lead her inside.

"Chris is fabulous," Molly told her. "In my opinion, he's the best stylist in the city. And the masseuse here has hands of gold. She's just the best. She'll have you feeling so relaxed, you'll feel you've melted right into the massage table."

"You come here?" Cindy asked, surprised that Molly could pay for such luxury on her salary.

Molly gave a little shrug. "I wouldn't call myself a regular customer," she said, "but I have been here a few times."

Cindy was left thinking, yet again, that there was more to Molly than she was willing to reveal.

Even though it was a weekday, and in Cindy's mind a *work*day morning, the spa was bustling with activity. The hair salon, located just behind the half wall at the rear of the waiting area, had several customers in various stages of the styling process. A young woman carried a neatly folded pile of fluffy white towels down the hall toward the back of the building. The salon/spa phone was ringing, so the receptionist, looking quite chic in her maternity business suit, smiled a quick greeting and told Cindy and her small entourage to have a seat. She then answered the incoming call.

The four women settled themselves, and Rachel commented, "This place is really busy this morning."

Suddenly all eyes were on Olivia as she picked up a magazine from the end table and began fanning herself with it. "Whew," she said. "I don't know if it's all the excitement, or what, but I'm not feeling so well."

Cindy did think Olivia's face was too pale. She started to say just that, but Olivia's eyes widened, her hand pressing to her stomach.

"I need to find the rest room." Olivia bolted from

her chair and then dashed out of the lounge in the direction the receptionist pointed.

"That flu is really getting to her," Molly said.

Rachel watched the empty doorway. "It's funny, though, that she hasn't suffered any other flu symptoms. A cough, or the sniffles."

A few minutes later, Olivia returned looking paler than ever.

"I lost my breakfast," she told them miserably. She sat down, swiping her fingers across her damp forehead.

"Here, try one of these." The receptionist approached them, a small bag of saltine crackers in her hand. "I keep them in my desk drawer. The bland taste helps settle my stomach." Her mouth cocked in an ironic grin. "They call it morning sickness, but I can get nauseated any time of the day."

Cindy remembered that the night of her birthday dinner, Olivia had tinged green at the sight of the guacamole dip. And she hadn't had anything to drink except water. Now here it was, two days later, and Olivia was still feeling sick. Molly was right, that stomach flu really did have a tight hold on Olivia.

Unwittingly, Cindy's gaze fell on the pregnant receptionist, one hand holding the package of crackers, the other maternally settled on her slightly rounded tummy. She smiled at the sight. Then Cindy looked at Olivia. Her friend nibbled the cracker she held in one hand—*her other nestled snugly on her lower abdomen.*

Blinking twice, Cindy felt her jaw go slack with the shocking thought. Could Olivia be...pregnant?

Could her nausea be caused because she's expecting a baby, rather than because she's contracted the flu?

Before she could give the idea another thought, a stylishly dressed woman came into the waiting area to collect her for her appointment.

"We're ready for you, Cindy," the woman said.

How on earth this woman knew exactly which one of them to address was a mystery to Cindy.

"B-but," Cindy said, feeling suddenly panicked for some reason, "what about Olivia? Maybe we should take her home. Maybe we should come back some other—"

"Oh, no," Olivia said. "I'll be fine. You go. Go right now. You're not missing this opportunity because of me."

"But," Cindy repeated.

"No buts." Rachel's tone was firm.

"We'll take care of Olivia," Molly told her. "In fact, we'll drive her home. It'll be hours before you're finished here."

"Hours?" Cindy's gaze was glued to Molly's face, but she felt the stylish woman take her by the arm and gently guide her away from her friends. "How many hours?"

"Just a few." A merry light danced in Molly's eyes.

Cindy allowed herself to be steered farther into the building. With her head pounding, her blood whooshing through her ears, she valiantly fought the enormous sensation that she was being led straight to the gallows.

* * *

"I've died and gone straight to heaven," Cindy had murmured softly twenty minutes into her massage. Molly had been right; the masseuse had hands that were worth their weight in pure gold.

Cindy had been rubbed and steamed in the sauna and scrubbed with a fragrant almond facial mask. Her entire body had been wrapped with seaweed—"To draw out the toxins" she'd been told. And Cindy hadn't even known she had any toxins. Then she'd soaked in a warm tub of mineral water. She'd been whisked from one phase of her total body makeover to the next, a fresh, fluffy towel waiting for her at the end of each.

Her nails—fingers and toes—had been trimmed and filed, buffed and polished. She'd murmured a protest when the manicurist had reached for a small bottle of ruby red gloss. Cindy had never painted her nails and wasn't sure she'd be comfortable with it, but she had been quickly informed that Molly and the others had requested the daring hue. In the end, she'd given a reluctant nod.

Soon she'd found herself in the styling salon. Her hair had been washed and cut, and then a lightening rinse had been applied.

"To bring out your beautiful golden highlights," Chris, the stylist, had told her in a reassuring voice.

With her damp hair wrapped in a towel, Cindy had a session with a cosmetologist. Cindy's eyebrows had been shaped, her skin moisturized, its tone evened out with foundation. Eyeliner had been applied, along with shadow, mascara and blush. The crowning touch had been the application of lipstick. However, before

Cindy was allowed to view herself in a mirror, she'd been hustled back to Chris who had dried and styled her new haircut.

Just a little over three hours after having entered the spa, Cindy was handed her glasses, which she slid onto her face, and then she was spun around to face the looking glass.

She gasped, stunned utterly speechless.

Her hair tumbled in soft curls to her jawline, tiny wisps framing her face. And the makeup. She'd been scared witless that the woman who had applied the color would go overboard, but Cindy was pleasantly surprised by how natural she looked. The eye makeup and blush simply enhanced her features rather than made them into some sort of bold statement.

Finally she let out her breath. That gorgeous woman staring back at her couldn't be Cindy Cooper, could it?

Suddenly she realized that a group of people had gathered behind her. She saw their reflections in the mirror. All the staff who had worked on her that morning were there: the masseuse, the seaweed-wrapping aesthetician, the manicurist and cosmetologist, and of course Chris, the hair stylist. They looked at her expectantly, each one gauging her reaction to their work.

Finally Chris tentatively asked, "You do like it?"

Cindy's gaze leveled once more on her reflection. *I don't really know,* she wanted to tell him. *I have no clue who that woman is staring back at me.*

You can't say that, a firm, silent voice chastised her. *These people have put a great deal of effort into this makeover. Your friends have paid good money for your time here.* Cindy knew what she had to do.

She smiled broadly. ''I look great,'' she told them. ''And I feel wonderful. All of you did a marvelous job.''

The Body Beauty Spa staff clapped and smiled, a couple of them voicing their approval of the changes that had been made. They obviously thought they had done a marvelous job, as well.

Cindy was hurried off to the changing room to slip back into her clothes. She kept glancing into the mirror every other second. She just couldn't help it. That woman looked so...*different.*

What would her friends say when they saw her? she wondered. What would they think? Would their treatment of her change?

Of course not! Molly and Olivia, Rachel, Sophia and Patricia had all pitched in for this makeover. They *expected* this metamorphosis.

But Kyle didn't. As Cindy smoothed her hand over the soft pleats of her long skirt, she couldn't help but wonder how he would react.

''Oh, my,'' Molly whispered.

''You're stunning,'' Rachel added.

Cindy felt herself blush as she stood in the lounge area of the spa, her friends giving her a thorough examination. They looked her over, head to foot, requesting a slow turn so they could get a complete view.

''Oh, my,'' Molly repeated.

''Stop,'' Cindy said, suddenly feeling self-conscious. "You'd think I was a toad turned into a princess, or something. It's still me."

I think. The words echoed through her head. She felt as though she were floating several inches above the floor. She felt…pretty. She knew she looked chic, fashionable, for the first time in her life.

A part of her wanted to feel disgusted with the happiness bubbling inside her. But she shoved the bad emotions away. She was determined to enjoy this gift, at least for a little while, before she let her dark feelings ruin it.

"The great part is," Cindy told them, "it's barely noon. I still have time to get back to Barrington and go over—"

"But we're not finished," Rachel said.

Molly chuckled. "That's right. We're not finished."

Cindy frowned. "What do you mean? What more can be done? I've been buffed and spiffed up—" she looked down the length of her and then grinned at her friends "—pretty much to perfection."

Rachel and Molly looked relieved and happy that Cindy was pleased with her visit to the spa. She was more than pleased, actually. Even though she knew she shouldn't be.

"Come on," Molly said. "We have another appointment."

"With my optometrist," Rachel revealed.

Cindy frowned. "B-but…"

Her friends hadn't listened to a word she'd said. Her arguments that she had her own eye doctor, that she'd just had her exam a few weeks ago and wouldn't need another for over ten whole months, had fallen on deaf ears.

"Dr. Henry is my eye guy," Rachel said. "He's agreed to fit you with a free pair of sample contact lenses. You'll love them."

"B-but…" Cindy had discovered that was her catch phrase of the day.

Forty minutes later, she was blinking her eyes, getting used to the contacts. Dr. Henry had expertly placed them in her eyes, and as she looked at herself in yet another mirror, she saw that his ministrations hadn't smudged her mascara or smeared her eyeliner.

"Lord," Rachel exclaimed, "look at the size of those green eyes you've been hiding."

"Oh, my," was all Molly was able to say.

Rachel smiled warmly at Dr. Henry, giving him her thanks, and then she and Molly hurried Cindy out the door and off they went. This time to the nearest department store.

Cindy found herself thrust into a fitting room and her friends brought her outfits to try on. Like a good little girl, Cindy donned each one, although these clothes were not to her usual taste. The colors were too bold, the styles too…tight. Too confining. Well, neither of these words was exactly right. The business suits Rachel and Molly chose were simply too *revealing* for Cindy's taste. The skirts were cut well above the knee. The jackets and tops had plunging necklines. Yes, they fit, and the clothes were comfortable enough. It was just that Cindy—

"I vote for this one," Molly said of the suit Cindy now had on. "Red just shouts 'Notice me!'"

"I liked the lime green one," Rachel said. "The color brings out your eyes."

Cindy perused her reflection in the three-paneled mirror. She felt an overwhelming urge to tug at the hem of the red skirt.

"I can't do this," she said. "I can't go to work dressed like a...like a floozy."

Rachel actually laughed. "A what?"

"This skirt is too short," Cindy complained. "And..." She paused, fanning her fingers at her chest. "And my boobs are hanging out."

She stood staring at herself. Suddenly she noticed that both of her friends had grown quiet. She slowly turned to face them.

Cindy was immediately aware of their hurt expressions.

"What?" she asked. "What did I say?"

"So you think we're floozies," Molly said quietly.

"We never knew you felt that way." Rachel crossed her arms over her chest.

Looking over the women, Cindy realized that the suits they had chosen for her resembled the ones they were wearing at the moment. But for some reason, their clothing didn't look quite as risqué as the suit she had on.

"I didn't mean that!" she cried. "I didn't mean that at all!"

Finally Molly could contain her grin no longer, and Rachel shook her head, laughing.

"We know you didn't," Rachel told her.

"You have to admit," Molly said. "You look downright sexy."

Spinning around to face her image in the mirror

again, Cindy clenched her fists. She really did, she decided. She did look sexy.

"You told us on your birthday that you felt you needed to do something drastic," Rachel reminded her. "Well, I think this is as drastic as you can get."

Her transformation was extreme. Very much so.

When Cindy had suggested she needed to change her situation, she had meant that she was thinking of putting Kyle out of her thoughts. She certainly had never imagined anything quite like this.

A quiet voice shimmered into her thoughts. What if the new Cindy could capture Kyle's attention?

Her heart fluttered against her ribs, the anticipation almost more than she could bear.

"I do want him to notice me," she whispered, knowing full well her friends would understand her meaning. "Desperately."

"Now there's no way he couldn't," Molly gently pointed out.

Rachel added, "You're going to knock the man completely off his feet."

Cindy lifted her chin and gazed at her friends through the mirror. Her decision made, she said, "I'll take the red suit. *And* the green one."

Molly and Rachel squealed their delight.

Reaching up to finger her soft, golden brown curls, Cindy sighed nervously. Kyle *would* notice her. That was almost a given, if she were to believe her dear friends. But she knew there would be some hefty problems waiting for her in the near future. The biggest problem would be coming to terms with the manner in which she was going to attract the attention of the man of her dreams.

Chapter Three

Cindy had hurried to the fourth-floor conference room when she'd returned to Barrington, intent on double-checking that everything for the presentation was ready. Patricia had done an excellent job in her absence, Cindy noted. The refreshments were displayed nicely off to one side of the room, a crisp white cloth covering the table. Colorful brochures lined the long oak table, one at each chair, along with pens and fresh legal pads in case the execs should decide to jot down information or questions during Kyle's presentation. The slide projector was plugged in, the bulb in working order, and the screen had been pulled down and secured in the open position.

Yes, Patricia had taken care of every detail. Still, Cindy had thought it prudent to check. However, doing so had taken twice as long as she'd expected. Every time someone passed the conference room they stopped to comment about her new appearance.

Heavens, one would think she *was* a toad-turned-princess.

Cindy's mouth curled into a saucy grin. She loved her new look. Absolutely loved her new hairstyle, her new clothes. She felt so different, so...*pretty*.

Why was it so hard for her to use that word?

Those construction workers outside the mall had certainly thought she looked good. Good enough that they hadn't been able to contain their wolf whistles. Her grin widened.

Normally she'd have been insulted by what, only yesterday, she probably would have described as offensive behavior, but she reminded herself that the men hadn't actually been whistling at *her*. They had been expressing their appreciation for the work that the people at the spa had done on her.

Still, Cindy couldn't lie to herself. She had kind of liked the attention.

When the first executives arrived in the conference room, Cindy greeted them warmly. And before either of them had a chance to catch her up in a long exchange regarding her makeover, Cindy excused herself and made for the nearest telephone. She punched in the four-digit number that would ring Kyle's office.

"Prentice," he answered.

The intense manner in which he spoke his name, the two short vowels fairly exploding off his tongue, the deep vibration of his tone, proud and confident, never failed to make her heart trip in her chest. She couldn't think of anything more appealing in a man than self-assurance. Unless it might be intelligence. Luckily Kyle had plenty of both.

"Everything's ready," she told him. "The execs are beginning to arrive."

"Great," he said. "Listen, I've been thinking. We can make a big impression by opening up this meeting just a little differently than we'd planned."

Without hesitation she eagerly replied, "I'm listening."

She was always thrilled by Kyle's creativity. When he tossed a thought at her, her own creative juices would begin to flow. The two of them worked well together, each bouncing ideas off the other, each adding their own special touch, elaborating and building, until the original idea was perfected. That was exactly how this new project had been born, through her and Kyle's teamwork.

"As soon as Mr. Barrington arrives," he said, "I want you to personally escort him to his seat at the head of the table. Then I want you to turn on the slide projector. I want a crystal-clear shot of the first slide projected on the screen. And then just see what happens."

"No introduction." It wasn't a question. She was simply working out his suggestion in her head. "Just let the image make its impact."

She instinctively understood where his idea was headed. She always had, even from the very beginning of their working relationship.

"I like it," she told him, her excitement growing.

"You think it's a good idea?"

"I do." She nodded, even though she knew full well he couldn't see her.

Then another idea formed in her head. "I'll turn down the lights. The slide will be clearer that way. But I'll leave them dim. I don't want you tripping on a chair leg when you make your way to the front of the room."

Glancing at the door of the conference room, Cindy said, "I'd better go. Mr. Barrington just arrived."

"I'll be there in half a minute."

Cindy's stomach was jumping with so much excitement she was sure she must have swallowed a entire troupe of tiny twirling acrobats. She felt a twinge as guilt stabbed at her. The dimming of the lights would allow a clearer image to be projected, but that wasn't the only reason she'd made the suggestion. If the lights were low, then at some point Kyle would have to ask her to brighten them. That was the moment she hoped to make her own impact. On Kyle.

Kyle slipped into the darkened conference room and actually smiled at the total silence. All eyes were trained on the computer-enhanced medieval castle that he and Cindy had worked so hard to create. He glanced at the back of the room where he knew Cindy was positioned at the slide projector, but the shadows were too deep for him to see her. Still, he lifted his hand and saw an indistinct movement as she returned his greeting.

The two of them had worked months and months' worth of long hours. He hoped the presentation went over well. If it didn't, it wouldn't be because they hadn't given it their all.

In his most dramatic voice, he said, "Imagine spending a night, or a weekend, or an entire week's vacation back in the Days of Knights. You step across the drawbridge and leave the twentieth century far behind. There will be jousting exhibitions, human chess matches, roaming bands of minstrels and troubadours. And every evening a grand banquet will be held. A banquet fit for a king." He grinned. "Or queen."

When he reached the front of the room, he turned to face his small audience of executive heads. "And you," he told them, "are treated like visiting royalty."

For several more moments he pitched the ideas that he and Cindy had concocted: costumed employees who were "in character" at all times, a truly Gothic experience that guests could become involved in, as much or as little as they chose. Barrington's Days of Knights would offer people a radical change from their everyday, *"present day"* lives.

"Now, I know you have questions regarding building costs, location and profit estimates," he said. "Let's roll up our sleeves and get down to business. Cindy, would you turn up the lights, please?"

The room brightened, and Kyle immediately sought to make eye contact with Cindy. He didn't know why exactly, but it seemed important to him to discover whether or not she was happy with his unveiling of Days of Knights. The idea was hers, too, and he wanted to know she was satisfied with how he'd presented—

The bold flash of red at the back of the room made him frown. And suddenly he was aware of one thing, and one thing alone. Legs. Shapely legs. A mile's worth of sensuous, womanly curves. High-heeled, sling-backed shoes showcased sexy ankles, the short skirt revealed firm calves, trim knees and well-proportioned thighs.

The sight was enough to make Kyle's mouth go dry as the Arizona air.

Time seemed to slow as his eyes meandered over slim hips, the narrow waist, settling for just a moment longer than necessary on the softly rounded breasts. The woman was a damned knockout! But who the hell was she? And what was she doing at his presentation?

Then another question echoed though his brain. Where was Cindy?

"Kyle, I love it!"

Mr. Barrington's booming voice made Kyle blink. He dragged his attention away from the unfamiliar female in the flaming red suit and focused his gaze on the president of the company—the man who had the power to accept or veto the new project.

"Cindy and I had hoped that you would," he told his boss.

Where the heck *was* Cindy? Kyle wondered, his gaze flying to the back of the room. She had called him from this very room to tell him that everyone was arriving.

The woman in red turned her head, the overhead

light catching and gleaming against the golden highlights in her softly curling hair. Then she smiled at
him, and Kyle made a stark realization. That was no
gorgeous stranger! That was his Cindy.

His Cindy? A tiny frown planted itself in his brow.
He'd never referred to her in such a possessive manner. Surely it was just the shock of seeing the extreme
change in her appearance.

He'd thought Rachel was simply taking Cindy to
have her hair done. Kyle never realized what a trip to
the beautician could do for a woman.

"Kyle?"

His heart slammed into high gear. *You're in the
middle of giving an important presentation,* he railed
at himself. *Pay attention, man.*

He spent the next few minutes going over the cost
figures and how he and Cindy had come up with
them.

Every other second, thoughts of Cindy flashed into
his head and he had to fight the urge to glance at her.
He was so relieved that he was well prepared for the
meeting. He'd predicted the questions that were being
asked of him, had even participated in a bout of role-
playing with Cindy to anticipate exactly what information might elicit queries.

Again her name whispered through his mind as he
thought about all the late nights they had spent working together on this project, and again he found himself wanting to dart a quick glance toward the back
of the room. This time he surrendered to the urge.

He'd never realized how large, how beautiful, how

vividly *green* her eyes were. They were utterly breath-taking. And so very expressive.

She's not wearing glasses, he noted for the very first time since realizing that the woman in red was actually Cindy. Was it really possible that, all the time he'd spent working with her, those glasses of hers had kept him from noticing how vivacious her eyes were?

No, he thought. He couldn't be completely dishonest with himself. He might have been taken totally off guard by the change in Cindy—a change he never expected—but it wasn't like he had no idea before this that she was a beautiful woman. He had known she was an attractive woman. Had even felt stirrings of desire for her. What red-blooded man wouldn't, working long hours with a such a woman?

His hard-and-fast rule against personal involvement had been what had kept him from acting on his feelings.

"I do have another question, Kyle," Mr. Barrington said.

Kyle focused his undivided attention on the owner of the company and waited.

"What have you planned that will keep guests coming back to Days of Knights?"

Smiling, Kyle commented, "An excellent question, sir. And since Cindy was the one who solved that problem, I'll ask her to take the floor on this one."

He and Cindy had talked about the dilemma of garnering the business of repeat customers. She had come up with an ingenious solution, and he had warned her to expect to be questioned on the subject, so he knew she was prepared.

Taking a more active part in the presentation was a great opportunity for Cindy, seeing as how her yearly performance review was due. But Kyle had to admit, offering her this chance to shine wasn't wholly unselfish on his part. No, he was eager to have a few uninterrupted moments while she was speaking to simply look at her.

"I thought," Cindy said, "that guests would be willing to return again and again to Barrington's Days of Knights if we had a small group of actors roaming the hotel and grounds. Actors who played key characters from history. One month they might reenact the turbulent story of Henry the Eighth and Anne Boleyn, another month, the times of George the Second, and his suppression of the Jacobite rebellion."

She smiled at Mr. Barrington, and Kyle felt his breath catch at the beautiful sight. His blood thickened with a sudden, gut-wrenching desire. He wanted Cindy. In the worst way. Kyle's only wish at the moment was that she'd bestow that gorgeous smile of hers on *him*.

Cindy went on answering questions from the other executives about her idea. Kyle had to smile at how well her concept was being received.

"History has given us years and years' worth of story lines to use," she summed up. "We'd never run out of new and interesting plots to reenact."

"Perfect," Mr. Barrington boomed. "History buffs from all over America would come to experience Days of Knights many times. This is just perfect!"

Mr. Barrington's praise made Cindy beam with pride. And if Kyle had thought her beautiful before, now she was dazzling. Her green eyes twinkled like jewels, her smile lit up the whole room. He couldn't help but notice that every eye was on her. Not one person was reading the brochure, or looking at him. Everyone was seemingly enthralled by Cindy.

"Well, I'm convinced," Mr. Barrington told the room at large. "I say we go ahead with the project. I think we should scout out a perfect location from the sites Kyle has suggested. And let's get some feedback from Accounting on the projected costs and profits." The man turned his attention to Kyle. "Congratulations! This is a great idea you and Cindy have come up with."

"Pardon me, Mr. Barrington," Cindy said.

Once again, Kyle watched as the room hushed and all eyes turned to his personal assistant. He felt a strange emotion creep over him. An emotion he had trouble identifying.

Possessiveness, he thought.

No way! he told himself. That wasn't what he was feeling at all.

Cindy said to Mr. Barrington, "It's been rumored that your son will be taking over the company when you retire. Is there any chance that he might cancel the project once he arrives in Phoenix?" Her face reddened and she blurted, "I mean, *whoever* takes over for you."

Kyle couldn't believe what Cindy had done. Yes, rumors *were* flying, but she should never have backed Mr. Barrington into a corner regarding his successor.

The whole atmosphere of the room changed. What had been an almost festive feeling transformed in the blink of an eye into tension. Every person in the room grew wide-eyed and waiting.

Before Mr. Barrington could speak, Mildred Van Hess said, "Cindy, Mr. Barrington's son hasn't yet agreed to come home from overseas."

Mr. Barrington leveled his gaze on Kyle. "But you can be assured," he said, "that whoever takes over the reigns of Barrington Corp. will know just how much I like the idea of Barrington's Days of Knights." The gray-haired man pushed out his chair and stood up. "Now, I say we all have a cup of coffee."

It was like the entire room took a deep breath. The men and women got up, some gathering to talk in small groups, some going to the refreshment table, and other's moving to address either Kyle or Cindy.

Kyle spent several moments talking to two different department heads about the new project. They congratulated him and then went to have some coffee. He glanced toward Cindy and his jaw clenched in a knee-jerk sort of reaction at what he saw.

She was surrounded by men. Kyle listened as they laughed and chatted, and he felt that odd emotion steal over him once again.

Jealousy?

Ridiculous!

Suddenly Cindy looked up and their gazes connected. Lingered. *Locked.*

The expression on her face couldn't be described as a smile. His skin prickled all over as her green eyes threatened to swallow him whole.

What the hell was going on? he wondered.

Still, she continued to stare. And then, oh so slowly, she let her eyes rove over his entire body, from head to foot and back again. The prickle he felt just moments before turned into a full-fledged flush. She couldn't have made him hotter if she'd reached out and run her fingers down the length of him.

Was it possible that Cindy was actually flirting with him?

No. He just couldn't believe that. Cindy would *never* do such a thing. He must be reading her wrong.

A silent voice inside his head barked out a humorous laugh. How can a man misread signals that strong? it asked.

Kyle had no answer. But he just couldn't accept the idea that Cindy would— No, he was mistaken. Terribly mistaken.

However, as much as he might like to think this wasn't happening, he simply could not deny what was smoldering low in his gut—a desire so blistering, it threatened to burn a hole right through him.

Cindy was quaking in her brand-new spike-heeled shoes. What on earth was she *thinking?* What in heaven's name was she *doing?* What had possessed her to offer Kyle those lingering, come-hither looks?

It was the makeover the girls had given her. The makeover had turned her into someone new. Someone unfamiliar. Someone willing to take risks. Big risks. Big, *sexy* risks.

The attention she was getting for some of these guys hadn't hurt. In the last twenty minutes since Mr.

Barrington had announced their Days of Knights idea a success, Cindy had received two invitations to lunch, one request for a dinner date and yet another for a night out on the town. The old Cindy had never experienced such ardent fascination from men before. The attention she was getting was inducing such... confidence. More than she could handle, it seemed.

And it wasn't as if she'd plotted and planned the looks she'd given Kyle. She'd simply glanced up, found him looking her way and wham, the next thing she knew the two of them were engaged in a bout of silent yet heated flirtation. Spontaneous seduction. That's how she'd describe it.

Heck, she didn't want to think about the "whys" and "how comes." She hadn't felt this uplifted, this *alive,* since those awful, dreary birthday blues had taken hold of her days ago. She was having too much fun to examine her actions too closely.

The room was thinning out now. Mr. Barrington and Mildred had already bid Cindy a good day, congratulating her yet again on the successful birth of a truly great idea. The two remaining execs were taking a final opportunity to shake Kyle's hand. Cindy's heart was pounding as she lifted a farewell hand to them as they took their leave. Finally she was alone in the conference room with Kyle.

He stood by the refreshment table, just looking at her, an unreadable expression in his mahogany eyes. Moistening her suddenly dry lips, Cindy prayed that he would come to her because she seriously doubted that her shaky knees would support her weight if she tried to walk.

After what seemed like an eternity, Kyle set down his coffee cup and slowly made his way across the room. The silence seemed deafening, and the giddy feeling in her stomach increased with every step he took. The oxygen in the air seemed to grow more compact, more difficult to breathe, the closer he came.

He stopped when he was just a tad closer than arms' reach.

"I want to congratulate you."

His voice was rich and smooth, like warm velvet caressing her skin. Of all the felicitations she'd received, Kyle's meant the most. To know he thought she performed well during her portion of the presentation meant the world to her.

A slow smile pulled at her mouth, and she didn't fight it.

"I mean," he continued, "I really—"

He reached out and encircled her forearms with his fingers, the heat of him penetrating the fabric of her suit.

"*—really—*"

Cindy's breath caught in utter surprise as he pulled her against his chest, bundled her up into his arms until his face was a hairbreadth from hers.

"—want to congratulate you."

Before she had time to think, to inhale, to close her eyes, his mouth was on hers.

Hot, needy, demanding.

Her mind was under attack; total chaos fought back all thought, scuffled with logic, clashed with reason.

So Cindy did the only thing she could. She surrendered to the turmoil. Totally.

Snaking her arms around his neck, she splayed her hands on his back. If she thought her knees had been weak before, now they were wobbly as warm rubber. But he was strong, and she held on tightly.

The feel of his hard body against hers was everything she'd ever dreamed it would be. Better, even, if that were possible.

The heated, woodsy smell of his cologne filled her nostrils, her lungs, sending sparks flying inside her— sparks that flashed and glittered bigger and brighter than any fireworks display she'd ever seen in her entire life. She wanted to touch him. To feel his skin against her.

Drawing her arms downward, she let her fingers trail over his jaw, down his neck and, farther still, to his chest. She felt his heart beating under his dress shirt, the furious thud driving her deeper into the chaos that reigned in her mind.

Parting her lips, she invited him to deepen the kiss. And he accepted her silent request. His tongue tasted and teased, and Cindy was barely able to suppress the whimper of need gathering at the back of her throat.

With a groan, Kyle pulled himself away from her.

Disappointment struck her like a slap and she actually gasped. She looked at him, her fingers lifting to touch her still-moist lips.

''I guess I should apologize, but…''

Kyle's words trailed, his ragged whisper infused with the obvious desire still pulsing through him.

''I don't know what you did.'' He reached up and

took a golden curl between his fingers, lifted it to his nose, then to his lips. "But you're damned beautiful."

Cindy's eyes widened at his statement. Humiliation, as cold and heavy as a wet wool blanket, fell on her shoulders. She dropped her hands to her sides.

Why are you hurt? a tiny voice silently asked. *Didn't you allow yourself to be painted up and preened over? Didn't you get fitted for contact lenses? Didn't you choose a brand-new, short and daring outfit?*

Didn't you do all of these things just to capture Kyle's attention?

She had no other choice but to murmur her thanks. His compliment should have made her happy. Should have overjoyed her. It's what she'd been wanting to hear from him for months. Well…it was almost what she'd been wanting to hear.

Yes, his appreciation should have pleased her. But it didn't. And she knew exactly why.

She felt an awkwardness slither and coil between them and she wondered if Kyle noticed it.

"The meeting went well," she said, hoping to spur some praise from him for her part in the presentation.

He nodded, but remained silent. Had he even heard what she'd said? Or was he too preoccupied with noticing all the changes in her?

The backs of his fingers were warm as he slid them down the curve of her jaw, and Cindy had to fight the urge to tilt her head into his touch.

When it looked like he was about to kiss her again, Cindy nearly panicked. She wanted to step away from him. She wanted to put a little space between them.

Are you insane? the voice shouted at her. *This is what you wanted. To be in Kyle's arms. To feel his hands on you. His lips on yours.*

"Not like this." Her breathy whisper was barely audible and she felt tears prickle her eyelids in tiny pinpoints of pain. But she wouldn't cry.

"What?" he asked softly, his eyes still roving slowly over her face, her hair.

"Nothing," she quickly answered. Then she repeated, "Nothing at all."

Suddenly she was absolutely frantic to know that he thought she was smart. That he thought she was creative and talented. That he thought she was a viable, important part of their team of two. Cindy just had to hear that he appreciated her for more than simply the makeup and glitter she wore.

A test! The desperate thought barreled into her brain with all the gusto of a runaway locomotive. She needed to test him. What she needed was to force him to tell her what she meant to him. In a purely professional sense.

She stepped away from him, and she saw a shadow of frustration cloud his eyes. He looked like a little boy who had just had his brand-new toy swiped right out of his hands. Something inside her froze, and she was more determined than ever to make him admit her professional value.

What better way to discover his opinion of her significance to him than to force him to think about losing her? Immediately, the rumors of the Third coming to Phoenix echoed into her brain. Before she could even fully formulate the idea churning into her head, it was spilling off her tongue.

"I've been wondering," she said in a rush. "If Mr. Barrington's son does take over the corporation, I'm sure he's going to need a personal assistant of his own. Do you think I'd be a good candidate for the job?"

She felt her face flush hot with anxiety. Surely he would tell her she was an excellent personal assistant, and that he'd hate to see her leave the New Products division.

Kyle's gaze turned cold and a muscle in his jaw tensed as he clenched his teeth together. If she didn't know better, she'd say he looked angry, and that confused her.

"So *that's* what this is all about?" he said.

Her brow creased with a frown. He *was* angry. But why?

"Wha—"

"You go out and get yourself all dolled up," he said, "with a little rouge and a little lipstick, and you think you can entice me to recommend you for a job promotion."

Cindy shook her head, her newly cut and curled tresses swinging against her cheeks. "No, Kyle, that's not—"

"And how dare you jeopardize *my* presentation," he plowed ahead, growing more furious by the moment, "by confronting Mr. Barrington about his successor. I can't believe you used my meeting as a platform to help you climb the corporate ladder. You don't ask about rumors and innuendos in a room full of executive heads. Your self-serving motives could have endangered the entire project.''

His presentation, was it? Cindy raised her chin a fraction as red-hot anger glowed inside her like burning embers. *His* meeting?

Again his jaw tensed. "We're just lucky that Mr. Barrington didn't rise to your bait. We're damned lucky he liked the idea.''

Cindy narrowed her eyes at him. "Kyle..." She let the rest of her thought fade. She paused long enough to take a deep, shaky breath. She didn't think she'd ever been so furious in her life.

How dare she? he'd asked. How dare *he?* How could he accuse her of using the presentation to further her career?

"We're just damned lucky," he said, "Mr. Barrington was good enough to overlook your blunder and give Days of Knights the thumbs-up.''

Swallowing around the hot, hard lump in her throat, Cindy picked up the file folder that held her presentation notes. Then she glared at him.

"Luck—" she ground out the words through gritted teeth "—had absolutely nothing to do with it. You—and I—worked hard on this idea. And it was a good one. No, it was a *great* one. That's why Mr. Barrington liked it. And if you had the smallest inkling of who I am, you'd know I'd never use a business meeting to—" She couldn't even finish the sentence. "You have no idea what the hell you're talking about.''

Without wasting another second, she pivoted on her brand-new spiked heels and marched out of the room.

Chapter Four

Cindy stared out her office window. The landscape surrounding Barrington Corp., the same one she usually found serene in its stark beauty, today seemed quite desolate and barren. Loneliness seemed to palpitate from the sunlit, sandy surface. She knew the difference in her feelings regarding the Phoenix desert vista was all due to her state of mind.

In all the time that she'd worked with Kyle, a harsh word had never been spoken between them. Now she felt afraid as she thought about their acrimonious exchange. She couldn't really call their angry dialogue an argument as, thank goodness, she'd stormed from the conference room before it had escalated to that level. However, she was frightened that, in that moment of quick retorts, their relationship had been forever changed.

And it was all her fault.

Why had she become so bent out of shape by his

attentive behavior? Lord, the mere memory of his kiss still made her heart *ka-thunk* in her chest like the persistent beat of some sensual, primeval drum. If only she'd remained coolheaded about his seductive manner. If only she hadn't been so blindsided by his kiss, his compliments. If only she hadn't panicked....

She groaned under her breath, laying her forehead against the thick glass window. Why had she felt the need to test him? Why had she insinuated that she was thinking of taking another job? For Barrington Corp.'s new president, no less. Had she completely lost her senses?

Yes came a swift and silent answer. But then, Kyle seemed to do that to her lately.

All her silly challenge had accomplished was to make him feel threatened. And worse than that, he'd misconstrued the whole situation. Kyle had added together the change in her outward appearance, her question to Mr. Barrington regarding his successor and her idiot-minded suggestion that she might consider taking the position as the new president's personal assistant, and he'd come up with an equation that couldn't have been more wrong.

Her makeover had been a gift from her friends, plain and simple. Her question to Mr. Barrington had been for the good of the new project, nothing more. And her stupid intimation of a promotion had only been a ploy to get Kyle to admit what he felt about her—a ploy that had backfired abominably.

Cindy absently tapped the palm of her hand with the eraser of a pencil. She could kiss goodbye any thoughts of a personal relationship with Kyle. Heck, if his cool treatment of her over the past couple of workdays since the presentation was any kind of gauge, then it looked as if she had pretty much destroyed the wonderful working alliance they had shared up until now.

She wished she could explain. She wished she could make him see that he misunderstood what had happened at the meeting.

The windowsill came into sharp focus when she blinked several times. Sudden excitement slammed through her like a bolt of lightning. Of course! That's exactly what she had to do. She had to explain. Tossing the pencil onto her desktop, she made for the door.

Cindy barged into Kyle's office without even knocking. He was dictating a letter into his voice recorder, and Cindy knew the tape would later be sent to the typing pool to be keyed into a computer and printed out. Kyle had never liked the idea of having a private secretary, preferring instead to answer his own phone calls and file his own papers. That way, he'd said more than once, if a document became misplaced or a phone call was mishandled, he'd have no one to blame but himself. However, papers were never mislaid in his office. He was much too obsessively organized for that. And contacts and business associates who called were always given top priority. Kyle was too much the professional to treat people any other way.

Placing her palms flat on his desktop, she leaned toward him. "We need to talk."

She knew everything about her body language expressed urgency—from her stiff, square shoulders, to the nervous tension she felt framing her mouth, even her wide eyes. She wanted to relax, to remain calm, but too much depended on her getting this right. Too much depended on her making him understand.

Kyle's gaze never wavered from hers as he snapped off his voice recorder. He didn't move. He simply sat there, silent and listening.

For an instant, and an instant only, his mouth was the sole object of her attention. She remembered his knee-melting kiss and the heated desire he had sparked to life in her. But she quickly and efficiently shoved the memory aside.

She thought she detected a wariness in his deep brown eyes. But she was too full of steam to ponder for long what he might be feeling.

"*I* need to talk," she clarified. "And I need for you to listen."

He continued to stare at her, motionless—seemingly *e*motionless—and she felt a startling trepidation creep over her skin in a wave, like an army of scampering mice. However, she ignored her anxiety. She had to press on. Her very career could hinge on what she was about to say.

"I want you to know," she began, "that I never had any intention of taking another job. Promotion or no promotion."

No response.

"I'm happy right where I am." She nervously raked her fingers through her wavy curls, the action only causing one tendril to bounce right into her line of vision. Swiping at it, she continued, "I'm content doing exactly what it is I'm doing."

Working with you. The words whispered through her mind, but luckily she successfully suppressed them. That kind of confession had no place here.

"The New Products division is right where I want to be," she stressed.

His statuelike countenance made her stomach more jittery than ever.

"I insinuated that I'd consider a new position be-cause—" she faltered "—because—" She pressed her lips together.

Because I wanted to force you to admit that you enjoyed working with me, she thought. *I tested you because I needed to know that your behavior toward me, your kiss, was due to more than merely my new outfit, my new hairdo, my new look.*

She couldn't say that! She'd be a fool to admit that. He'd laugh her right out of his office.

A reason. A reason. She needed a rational expla-nation for what she'd done. For the things she'd said.

Her mind whirled a mile a minute. Then an idea came to her.

"I mentioned the new personal assistant's posi-tion," she said, setting up her little white lie, "be-cause I was really pushing you for your opinion re-garding my work. I knew you'd be filling out my yearly review this week, and I wanted to know your appraisal of me. You know," she quickly added, "as an employee."

As soon as she'd used her yearly review as a jus-tification she realized how very flimsy her story sounded. Well, it was only a small lie. She *was* due for her review. And she *was* interested in his evaluation of her career accomplishments.

Kyle rested his elbow on the arm of his leather chair, then he settled his chin on top of his crooked fingers, perusing her all the while. What was he thinking? she mused. What was going through his head? Did he believe her?

"You flirted with me."

His words were slow and deliberate, not an accusation as much as a simple statement of fact.

Awkwardness stiffened the air, and Cindy averted her gaze self-consciously. She couldn't deny the blatant truth. She had teased him from across the conference room. But she blamed her makeover. The new clothes, the new makeup, had made her...indiscreet. Not just indiscreet, she decided suddenly. Her makeover had made her outrageously bold.

No, she couldn't deny her behavior, couldn't deny her flirtation, but she didn't have to acknowledge it, either...so she said nothing.

"You've come in here," he continued, "to explain that you didn't flirt with me the other day in order to get my recommendation for a promotion. That you're not interested in working as the new president's personal assistant."

"Exactly." Relief flooded through her. She was so glad that he seemed to understand her after all.

He nodded slowly as he continued. "But you are saying that you polished yourself all up and flirted with me to get a better yearly assessment."

Her gasp was audible. "Of course not! That's not what I'm saying at all."

Frustration and defensiveness made her flush red as a beet. She was completely flustered, and thoughts started rolling off her tongue, like water gushing over boulders in dangerous white rapids.

"My friends gave me this makeover as a *gift*," she said, her vulnerable position causing her to speak more harshly than she'd intended. "I'll have you know there was no other reason than that! And I only asked Mr. Barrington about his son's support of Days of Knights because I wanted to know the project wouldn't be cut...wouldn't be *killed* after Mr. Barrington retired. We've worked too hard to let that happen. And there's absolutely nothing wrong with an employee who tries to find out how her boss feels about her performance."

She was blubbering, she knew. Half-truths and white lies were twisting her up in knots. However, she was powerless to arrest the outpouring of words and emotions. But then she paused. Was that merriment gleaming in his eyes? Indignation struck her like a lightning bolt from the blue.

Her eyes narrowed accusingly. "Let's not forget that you kissed me. It's completely natural for a woman to want to find out why something like that would happen." Plunking her hands on her hips, she said, "I did *not* flirt with you to get a better performance review. The mere idea is ludicrous. Now, if you don't mind, I have work to do."

Cindy exited Kyle's office with as much grace as a lumbering pregnant elephant.

Darn it! she thought. She'd gone in there to make him understand. To smooth out all the rough spots of their working relationship. And all she'd ended up doing was creating more turmoil and making herself look even more like an idiot than she already did.

She'd bet a whole month's salary that Kyle hadn't believed a word she'd said. A sigh escaped her as she softly shut her office door. And she really couldn't blame him.

Kyle sat at his desk for longer than he cared to admit, pondering the scene that had just taken place in his office. He'd actually been pleased to see Cindy when she'd barged in on him. They had scarcely exchanged two words since their argument the day of the presentation. And she'd been on his mind incessantly since they'd shared those heated words…that heated kiss. The memory of those few passionate moments had filled him with hot desire. So much so that he'd been barely able to work. Barely able to think.

She'd come to make peace, he'd known that. And he couldn't quite figure out why he'd goaded her. But the color that had burned in her cheeks had been irresistible. As was the exasperation that had flashed in those gorgeous green eyes, the same eyes that stubbornly continued to haunt his dreams.

He shoved the thoughts from his brain. He couldn't allow such ideas to linger in his head. He simply couldn't.

But he continued to sit at his desk, ever so slowly drumming his index finger on the smooth oak as he became embroiled in figuring out the intriguing puzzle of her seemingly confused tirade just now. What was the meaning behind all the things she'd said? he wondered.

She'd proclaimed that her makeover was a gift from her friends. A gift and *nothing more than that*.

A small grin curled one corner of his mouth as he easily imagined her stomping her foot in childish frustration. He couldn't help but question if maybe the change in her wasn't as simple as she so obviously wanted him to believe.

Let's not forget that you kissed me.

His smile widened as he remembered the accusation glittering in her jewel eyes. Oh, but she was a beautiful woman. Her curious comment about it being natural for a woman to find out why a man would kiss her nibbled away at his thoughts.

Oh, he'd kissed her all right. And it wasn't something he was likely to forget for a long time to come, no matter how hard he might try. That kiss had been invading his dreams, making them torturous and leaving him tossing and turning in his lonely bed night after long night.

Again he cut the thought to the quick. He couldn't afford to entertain such thoughts. It just wasn't safe. Not after what he went through before.

Get busy, he ordered himself. *Think about something. Anything.*

Although knowing full well he had plenty of work needing to be done, several phone calls needing to be made, he continued to sit there, pondering.

Wrapping her hands around the steaming mug of coffee, Cindy sighed. "I'm feeling so confused."

Olivia set down the saltine cracker she was nibbling. "I'm sorry," she said. "Is there anything we can do?"

Cindy shook her head. "I don't think there's anything anybody can do. Every day I come to work, things between me and Kyle seem to grow more…strange."

"From what you've told us—" Patricia rested her hands on the break room table "—I think the situation is more *strained* than strange."

There were nods of agreement around the table.

A delighted chuckle bubbled from Molly. "Don't be so glum, you guys. Sometimes strained is good." Her hazel eyes danced. "It all depends on what's causing the strain. Now tension caused from anger is bad, *but*—" she grinned "—tension caused from sexual attraction…now that's good." She waggled her brows suggestively.

"So I guess we need to discover the exact cause of the strain between Cindy and Kyle," Olivia said.

"And here I thought that makeover had started him off with a bang," Sophia said to the others, "seeing how he kissed her."

Cindy felt her skin grow warm with the mere mention of Kyle's kiss. Goodness, how she'd dreamed about his mouth on hers. And the girls had been giddy with excitement when she'd told them about it. But she'd quickly assured them that the kiss hadn't meant a thing. Not a thing.

"Maybe she shouldn't have confronted him like she did," Rachel said.

Cindy noticed how her friends, one by one, leaned

forward a little as they discussed her situation. She really liked the fact that they were so concerned. It meant they cared. But it would have been nice to be included in the conversation.

"Well, she had to do *something*." Olivia paused long enough to sip her ginger ale. "She couldn't let him go on believing she was thinking of leaving her job."

"Oh, I don't know about that," Molly piped up. "Sometimes it's good to keep a man in the dark."

Rachel smiled as she shook her head. "You and your good things and bad things. And what, may I ask, makes you the expert?"

Molly simply laughed in reply.

"Well," Sophia said, "if someone were to ask me what Cindy should do, I'd say—"

"Pardon me, ladies," Cindy softly interrupted, "but you've been talking about me like I'm not here."

There were several murmured apologies, and then Rachel said, "Well, tell us what you think is going on in Kyle's head."

Cindy actually groaned, locking her gaze onto her coffee mug. "That's what has me so confused. I was sure he was angry with me. But ever since I barged into his office to try to explain things to him, he's been…different."

Noticing the quiet, Cindy looked up at her friends. The eager expectation they expressed—so obviously waiting for her to elaborate—would have made her laugh if she wasn't feeling so darned miserable.

"He's continuing to act pretty standoffish toward

me," she told them. "And that's what has me be
lieving he's still angry. But…" She hesitated, fretting
over making more of what was on her mind than she
should.

"But what?" Rachel gently prodded.

"Well, I *feel* him looking at me," Cindy confessed.
"I feel his eyes on me whenever we're in the same
room. I feel this strong…electricity." She shook her
head, feeling silly. Then she sobered. "I'm sure he's
staring at me. Studying me. And I'm not sure why."

"Not sure why?" Molly's tone rose just a bit. "It's
because there's so much more to look at now."

Cindy knew her friend was talking about the makeover. Since her two odd and troubling incidents with
Kyle, Cindy had considered reverting back to her old
look: wearing her long, flowing skirts and her glasses,
and brushing the soft, full curls from her hair. But she
hadn't.

"I do have to admit," Rachel said, "I'm a little
surprised that you've gone on wearing your new
clothes, your makeup and contacts. I mean, after
things went so wrong after the presentation and you
and Kyle ended up arguing—"

"But why shouldn't she look good?" Molly asked.
"She's thirty years old. She can't let some man dic-
tate how she should dress."

Cindy only wished she had Molly's spunk. Guilt
pinched her heart as she whispered, "I do like it. I
like being the object of Kyle's attention."

"Honey," Olivia said, reaching out to touch her
wrist, "you're talking like there's something wrong
with you enjoying the fact that Kyle is noticing you."

The idea that Kyle was staring at her, noticing her, was the only reason she hadn't gone back to her old style of dress. It bothered her more than she could admit to think that her physical appearance was the only reason behind Kyle's interest. But the girls wouldn't understand why she was bothered by that thought. They just wouldn't, so she didn't try to explain. The best thing to do was change the subject.

"But what if I've got it all wrong?" she asked them, her tone expressing the idea that she was sure she did. Cindy thought about how the air actually seemed to snap and spark whenever she was with Kyle now. The feeling was so strong. But she was simply too afraid to hope, too afraid that she was imagining everything. "What if he isn't staring at me with interest? What if he's glowering at me because he's still angry?"

Shy Patricia leaned forward, her voice tentative as she said, "There is one way to find out." All eyes turned to her. "You could accept some of those dinner invitations you've been receiving from other guys in the office."

Cindy frowned, not quite understanding Patricia's advice.

"Fantastic idea, Patricia!" Molly exclaimed. "She's right, Cindy. You need to make Kyle jealous."

An uncomfortable prickling sensation swept over her. Oh, she couldn't do something like that. That kind of behavior too closely mirrored what she'd grown up around. Besides, she'd already made the big mistake of testing Kyle.

"I'm not so sure that would work," she told Molly and Patricia. She hated to hurt their feelings, but she just couldn't see herself involved in any more immature games. Again she tried to change the subject. "You know, I've tried for months to get close to Kyle. I've been wondering if maybe something happened in his past. Something that has made him... distrustful. Unable to give his heart."

"Oh, he doesn't distrust women," Molly declared. "He's just playing hard to get. Men do that sort of thing all the time."

Seeming to sense Cindy's discomfort, Rachel tossed her a sympathetic look.

"Speaking of men," Rachel said, "have any of you seen that new guy? The one who's been delivering the mail the last couple of days?"

"His green eyes are to die for," Patricia said.

"He is pretty cute," Olivia observed quietly.

Molly nodded. "He sure is. Tall, dark and handsome. And he's the perfect candidate to make Kyle jealous."

Cindy shook her head frantically, her eyes wide.

Laughter bubbled from Molly. "I'm kidding. I'm kidding."

Everyone chuckled, and concluding that Molly really was only teasing her, Cindy joined in.

Meaning only to add to the joking atmosphere, she said, "Tall, dark and handsome, huh? I'll have to check this guy out."

"Oh, you wouldn't want to date Mike, Cindy," Sophia said.

The strange quality in Sophia's voice had Cindy, and all the women, looking at the pretty blonde.

"You already know his name, Sophia?" Rachel observed.

Sophia's spine stiffened with what Cindy could only guess was self-consciousness.

"I do know his name," Sophia said defensively. "But only because he travels right past my desk when he's making his deliveries. But like I said, Cindy wouldn't want to date him, even if she *was* only looking to make Kyle jealous. No self-respecting woman would go out with Mike." Her voice lowered as she pointed out what seemed to her to be the obvious. "The man works in the mail room. How ambitious could he be?"

"We're only talking about dinner," Molly said. "Besides, she wouldn't actually have to go out with the man, she'd only have to…"

The remainder of Molly's comment went unsaid as the door to the break room opened and Kyle walked in. The group of women fell noticeably silent.

Cindy was acutely aware of how quiet the room was. Panic swept over her like a huge ocean wave. Her heart pounded, her pulse raced and the temperature of the room seemed to heat up by ten full degrees.

Kyle went directly to the large coffee urn and poured himself a cup. Still, the women remained mute.

Cindy felt quite desperate all of a sudden and looked at her friends, silently begging them to continue making small talk. She certainly didn't want

Kyle guessing that the prominent silence was due to the fact that he'd interrupted their conversation—the topic of which had been how to go about making *him* jealous. But as she looked from Rachel to Molly, then to Olivia, Patricia and Sophia, Cindy saw so much merriment lighting all their gazes, she was sure they'd burst into mischievous giggles at any moment.

They saw how uncomfortable she was feeling, she realized, due to Kyle's presence. And they were really enjoying her misery! She threw them all a covert glare.

Molly called out, "Hi, Kyle."

"Molly," Kyle greeted. He nodded toward the table, saying, "Ladies." His gaze zeroed in on Cindy as he crossed the few yards of tile floor between him and the table where they were all sitting.

There it was! That current. Those heated vibrations that seemed to suck all the air out of the room. Cindy wondered if her friends felt it, too.

"I haven't had a chance to talk to you this morning," Kyle said to her.

The rich timbre of his voice made the small hairs on the back of her neck stand on end. The intensity expressed in his penetrating brown eyes was such that she felt as if she and Kyle were the only two people in the break room.

"Are we still on for our two o'clock meeting?" he asked.

She nodded. "I was able to get your plane reservations for the time you wanted." Her voice sounded breathless to her own ears, and she could have kicked herself for not being more in control. "And the hotel—"

He stopped her with an uplifted palm. "Enjoy your coffee break. We can discuss the details this afternoon."

Again she gave a silent nod.

"Hey, girls—"

Molly's tone was loud enough to make Cindy start.

"—maybe Kyle can help us convince Cindy."

A frown bit deep into Cindy's brow. Convince her of what? Cindy frantically wondered. What the devil was Molly up to?

Her gaze darted to Molly's face, and Cindy was surprised and more than a little confused by the sudden, deep concern her friend seemed to be exhibiting.

"There's this new guy," Molly explained to Kyle. "He works downstairs—"

"In the mail room," Sophia was quick to supply.

Molly never lost a beat as she continued. "He's really interested in Cindy, and we're trying to get her to go out with him."

"I'm not doing this." The warning in Cindy's voice was clear, she thought. She had no interest in playing some game meant to make Kyle jealous.

"*We know,*" Patricia chimed in. "That's why we're trying to get Kyle to help us convince you."

Cindy gasped softly. Patricia had purposefully misinterpreted what she'd said. Her words had been twisted around to sound as though she was refusing to go out with Mike.

"He's a real cute guy," Patricia continued. "Isn't he, Olivia?"

With her eyes wide now, Cindy's looked at Olivia who seemed to be teetering on the edge of wanting to join in on the fun and staying out of the whole mess. Then Olivia smiled, her decision evidently made.

"He *is* cute," she said.

They were all against her! Cindy silently wailed. Then her gaze leveled on Rachel. No, not all of them, she told herself. Surely Rachel wouldn't let her be fed to these wolves she called friends. Tacit pleading was clearly written on her face as she looked at Rachel. However, Rachel's attention was focused on Kyle.

"Cindy says she can't go out with this guy," Rachel said, "because she's out of practice. She says she wouldn't know how to act on a date."

They *were* all against her! Every single one of them. Including Rachel. Cindy felt horrified by what her friends were doing to her. How was she ever going to face Kyle again? How was she ever going to explain?

However, what she didn't realize was that things were only going to go from bad to worse.

"You know, Kyle," Molly said. "This is all your fault."

What? Cindy was aghast.

"Cindy wouldn't feel so out of practice," Molly went on, "if you didn't keep her working such long overtime hours."

Patricia folded her fingers together, her face the epitome of innocence as she said to Kyle, "You know what would be nice? If you were to take Cindy out to dinner. You know, on a kind of pretend date. That

way she'd get a little practice in before she accepted
the dinner invitation from Barrington's new mailman.''

A pretend date? Where had Patricia come up with
that idea? And all this time Cindy had thought Patricia was shy and timid. Why, the woman was cunning
as a fox. By now Cindy's eyes were clenched shut
and her bottom lip was clamped firmly between her
teeth. All she wanted to do was curl up in a tiny ball,
slide right underneath the table and disappear.

She couldn't imagine how embarrassed Kyle must
feel. Well, on second thought, she knew just how embarrassed he must feel. Because she was feeling the
same. How was she ever going to face him at their
meeting this afternoon? Maybe she should just take
the afternoon off. Maybe she should put in for a trans-
fer. Maybe she should take what clothes she had on
her back and move to Outer Mongolia.

''I'd be more than happy to help Cindy.''

Three full seconds passed before she was able to
actually comprehend what Kyle had said.

''In fact,'' he continued, ''I'll take her to dinner
tonight. I hadn't realized that her overtime schedule
had been encroaching so badly on her social life. Is
seven o'clock okay with you?''

Near hysteria broke out in her brain when she realized that his last question had been directed at her.
What should she do? Should she blurt out the truth?
That there was no dinner invitation from Mike? That
the whole wild story was created as a means of making Kyle jealous, and it had snowballed out of control
until it included a suggestion that Kyle take her out?

Lord, she would never be able to explain this. Never.

Inhaling slowly, Cindy garnered all the control she could muster. She glanced up at Kyle and said, "Seven o'clock sounds good to me."

"Good," Kyle said. Then he said his goodbyes to the ladies and left the break room.

"Wow," Molly exclaimed, "did that turn out great, or what?"

Olivia laughed. "It couldn't have gone better if we'd have rehearsed it."

"And suggesting that pretend date was sheer genius, Patricia," Rachel said.

Patricia's face just beamed.

"How could you?" Cindy stood up and reached for her purse. "How could you guys do that to me?"

"Oh, now," Sophia crooned. "Calm down."

"You lied," Cindy accused them all. "You lied to Kyle."

"Well, just a little," Molly admitted. "But look at the bright side. Kyle's taking you on a date."

"A *pretend* date," she reminded them. "A pretend date that's based on a basket full of lies."

She glared at their grinning faces before she walked away.

"Now don't be angry with us," Rachel called after her.

"We did it for you," Olivia said.

Before the break room door swooshed shut, Cindy heard them all laughing triumphantly. But she was simply too upset to feel jubilant. She couldn't believe her friends would pull her into such a mess—a mess she'd now have to face all on her own.

She punched the elevator call button and waited. How was she going to straighten this out? she wondered, apprehension lying heavy in her stomach. But then something strange began to twirl and dance on top of the dark dread. Something light, almost buoyant. And it took Cindy the entire ride in the elevator up to the fourth floor to identify it.

Excited anticipation.

Chapter Five

Cindy stood at her closet, mentally debating on one outfit after another. This might be a *pretend* date she was going on with Kyle, but she still wanted to look her best.

She groaned softly. Nothing she owned seemed suitable. Granted, she didn't have many evening clothes to begin with. Why would she, when she spent all her time working at Barrington Corp.? But the dressy clothes she did have were part of her old wardrobe of unexciting, figure-hiding styles. Another soft groan escaped her. What was she going to wear?

Her two o'clock meeting with Kyle couldn't have been more awkward. Kyle had seemed quite unruffled by the scene in the break room when all her friends had railroaded him into taking her out to dinner. When she went to his office to discuss the details of his trip to California he seemed his business-as-usual self, but Cindy had been a bundle of raw nerves.

She'd left half of the information regarding the travel plans she'd made for him on her desk and she'd had to go and retrieve it. Then she couldn't seem to relay the airport shuttle times and plane schedules accurately. Oh, the plans she'd made for him were just as he'd requested. It was just that her nervous state made it impossible for her speak correctly or coherently.

Finally she'd simply handed him the file with all the schedules, connecting flights and hotel reservations and told him to look it over. All she wanted to do was get out of his office before he had a chance to bring up their date. And she'd almost succeeded.

She'd already pulled open his office door and had tossed a cursory goodbye smile over her shoulder.

"So I'll pick you up at seven," he had called after her.

Sudden anxiety had frozen her smile into something that felt—and most probably looked—plastic. "Seven sounds good," she had told him.

Cindy would have left then, but he said, "I'll need your address."

"Oh." She'd felt silly that she hadn't thought of it herself. "Of course."

She'd gone to his desk and jotted down her apartment number and street name on a piece of paper, realizing then that Kyle had never been to her home. She found it kind of sad to think that she'd never really seen this man—whom she cared for so very deeply—outside of Barrington Corp.

Before she had completed writing down the information, Kyle had said, "I haven't met this new guy from the mail room. The one who's interested in you."

Without a thought, Cindy had admitted, "Me, either."

Kyle's frown had made her nearly gasp. Lord, she'd been sure she'd ruined everything right then and there.

"You're going to go out with a man you've never even met?" There had been clear disapproval in Kyle's tone.

That had been her chance, she'd thought. To tell him the whole sordid truth. However, she'd let the moment slide. She wanted this date with Kyle. She might hate the circumstances surrounding it, she might feel terrible because of the lies, but she wanted this date. Just this one. Was that too much to ask?

"Y-you heard the girls rave about him," she'd stammered. "They say he's good-looking. And friendly." She'd shrugged, her plastic smile shining. "Besides, he apparently thinks I'm cute."

By then her anxiety level had been through the roof. She just had to get out of there before she lost her nerve and confessed everything.

"See ya at seven." She'd hustled out of his office and had spent the rest of the day deeply immersed in projection numbers and building costs so she wouldn't have to think about what she was doing.

Now here she was, searching frantically for something decent—and seductive—to wear on this date that she simply *had* to go on. Why had she been so stubborn this afternoon in Kyle's office? Why hadn't she just fessed up to the truth when she'd had the perfect opportunity?

Because you simply can't give up *this* perfect opportunity, a silent voice responded. A date. With the man of her dreams. Any woman would lie, cheat or steal to have a chance like this. It didn't matter if it was pretend or not.

Cindy reached to the very back of her closet and pulled out a plain, black cocktail dress. The scoopneck, long sleeves and A-line design equated a timeless style. Yes, the hem was a little long, coming to rest right at her knee, but she was sure a little feminine ingenuity could fix that problem.

After slipping the dress onto her body, she went to her dresser and pulled out a long, narrow scarf. The silky, diaphanous strip of fabric was so sensuous to the touch, when she'd received it from one of the girls this past Christmas, she'd wondered when she would wear such a thing. But now she saw that it was the perfect solution to her problem.

The fully lined dress felt smooth against her skin as she neatly folded the material at her waist and then secured the black silk scarf into place to hold it. There, she thought. That would hold the hem a couple of inches above her knee and show off her legs to their best advantage. Grinning, she couldn't help but feel like a teenaged Catholic school girl hiking up the skirt of her uniform. With her thoughts so focused on a certain oh-so-handsome male, Cindy guessed the extra leg she was intent upon showing just might have earned her a well-deserved rap on the knuckles with some disapproving nun's ruler.

She expelled a whispery chuckle as she fluffed her soft curls with her fingers and then looked in the mirror to check her makeup. Perfect, she thought. Well, as perfect as she was going to get, anyway.

The buzzer sounded, indicating that someone was at her front door. It was Kyle. The heady anticipation that had simmered in her stomach all afternoon now churned and spiraled, until she felt she had her very own mini tornado whirling out of control inside her.

Shoes! She needed shoes. Running for the closet, she pulled out a brand-new pair of black sling-backs, the three-inch heels designed to show off her shapely calves. Before she slipped her feet into them, she ran her hand up the length of her silk-stockinged leg.

The move had been completely spontaneous, made for the sole purpose of making sure her hose were smooth and properly positioned. But she wasn't prepared for the wave of memory-filled bleakness that rolled over her, swallowing her whole.

As a little girl, Cindy had watched her mother make that very same movement dozens—no, *hundreds*—of times before going out for the evening.

"This isn't the same thing," Cindy whispered to the empty room, dread sitting on her chest like a lead weight. "It isn't the same thing at all."

She reached up to push her hair from her eyes, and her own movement in the dressing mirror caught her eye. She looked at her reflection, the short and sexy haircut, the made-up face, the shorter-than-usual dress.

Are you certain this isn't the same thing? a small, stern voice whispered in her head.

Cindy wanted desperately to answer no. But she just couldn't be sure she was being completely honest.

The doorbell buzzed a second time, the sound continuing a little longer than it had the first time.

Shoving the silent doubts aside, she firmly said, "I want to do this. I want to go out on this date with Kyle."

Without reflecting any longer, without one more thought about the past, she snatched up her small evening bag and went to answer the door.

The single candle threw romantic light across the tabletop. Cindy dabbed at the corners of her mouth with a napkin and then smiled at Kyle.

"My dinner was delicious," she told him. "Thank you."

Her filet mignon had been prepared in a delicate and very yummy butter sauce. And the vegetables had been roasted to perfection.

"You're welcome," he said. "But we aren't finished yet. There's still dessert."

Automatically Cindy pressed her palm to her stomach. "Oh, I couldn't. But don't let me keep you from having something."

He smiled, and Cindy felt her heart lurch in her chest. The sensuous tension she'd felt between them for days and days now was very much present as they sat in the restaurant. However, she was getting used to it. In fact, she was finding she actually liked the heightened sense of awareness that the current—or electricity, or whatever it was—caused.

"I'm not much for sweets," he said. "How about coffee?"

She nodded. "Coffee would be wonderful."

As the waitress removed their empty plates and silverware and then poured them coffee, conversation lagged and Cindy took a moment to study Kyle.

He looked so handsome in his dark, double-breasted suit. Seeing him in a blazer was nothing new to her. He wore a suit every day at Barrington. But he was comfortable enough with her to loosen his tie, remove his jacket and roll up his shirtsleeves whenever they worked past five. And by that time of the day, his jaw was usually shadowed with a new growth of whiskers, although she had to admit she found the rugged look very sexy indeed. But tonight he'd shaved before picking her up, his face looking so smooth, it was all she could do to keep from reaching out and running her fingers over his skin.

Kyle looked just as polished and shined as she did with her new makeover. A smile stole across her mouth and happiness danced in the pit of her stomach. She liked the idea that he'd gone to such pains to look so good. Just for her.

After taking a sip from his coffee cup, he said, "You know, all through dinner we talked about work. Days of Knights, my upcoming trip to California, the renovation plans for the older hotels."

He looked at her for a silent moment, then continued. "If you go out—" He stopped, a small frown drawing his brows together for an instant. Then he amended, "*When* you go out with this guy from the mail room, you're going to have to tell him about yourself. The conversation is going to have to become, you know, a little more personal.''

A chuckle emanated from deep in his chest, a sound that Cindy found to be extremely sexy. She'd have loved the opportunity to place the flat of her hand on his chest and feel the vibration of his laughter against her palm. However, she knew that wasn't something that was going to happen any time soon. And it would never happen if he ever got wind of the big fat lies she and her friends had told him.

''What's funny?'' she asked.

His dark eyes glittered, and Cindy's whole body seemed to grow warm at the sight.

''Not funny, really,'' he said. ''Peculiar would be a better description.''

She grinned. ''Then what's so peculiar that it has you laughing?''

He moistened his lips, and Cindy's eyes were glued to the slow path the tip of his tongue made across his dusky flesh. The memory of their kiss in the conference room flashed through her mind, and her blood heated even more.

That kiss had been so quick. Too quick. She wondered what it would be like to have lots and lots of time to feel his mouth on hers. Time to experience him. Time to taste him.

''In all the time we've worked together,'' he said, ''we've never sat down and talked about ourselves. I don't know a thing about you. I don't know where you were born, where you grew up, where you went to school. Nothing.''

He ran his index finger down the length of his coffee cup, and something happened to the atmosphere. It grew taut. Like elastic, or a big rubber band that had been stretched tight.

After a moment she said, "I don't know a thing about you, either."

The sultry quality of her voice startled her. She wondered if Kyle heard it.

Reaching out, he slid his fingers over the back of her hand, his thumb resting in the valley between her first two knuckles.

"I'll tell you what," he said, "you tell me about you. Then I'll tell you about me. Deal?"

She smiled. "Deal."

So over a leisurely cup of coffee, she told him she was born in New York, that she'd grown up in various big cities all over the world. London, Paris, Houston, Los Angeles, Montreal. She'd even lived in Melbourne, Australia, for eighteen months as a teenager. As to her education, she went to school wherever she happened to be at any given time.

Kyle's dark eyes lit with fascination, just like everyone else who had ever listened to Cindy speak of what they saw as a different and exciting adolescence. What Cindy never told anyone, and she would not tell Kyle now, either, was that she hated her childhood. She abhorred growing up with no sense of permanence in her life. Never knowing where she would be during any given month, never knowing when she'd have to pick up and move.

That sort of life-style created two different types of people. Outgoing extroverts who made friends easily, or reserved introverts who had a hard time meeting people.

Cindy placed herself in the latter category. Lighting from place to place had made her terribly shy. Not to mention lonely. It seemed that just as soon as she'd made a friend or two, she would be flying off to some other corner of the world.

As far as she was concerned, her childhood might have been different all right, but there had been nothing exciting or interesting about how she'd grown up. The worst part had been the men. All those men. And not one father for her among them.

No, it just wouldn't do to go into too much detail with Kyle.

"Enough about me," she finally told him. "Tell me about you."

By then the small band had begun to play and several couples were enjoying the music as they slowly circled the parquet dance floor.

"Dance with me." Kyle reached out and took her hand, standing up at the same time.

Although she allowed him to guide her from her chair, she felt panic well up like a tidal wave. Cindy frantically blurted, "Don't think I'm going to let you get out of our deal. I held up my end. You need to hold up yours."

She felt she was filling the air with meaningless words, but she couldn't help it. The idea of being in Kyle's arms as they swayed to what held the promise of being the most romantic music ever created was enough to totally unnerve her.

He chuckled, and again she felt the urge to splay her hand on his chest, but again she resisted.

"I'm not trying to get out of anything," he told her. "We can talk and dance at the same time, can't we?"

His boyish grin was charming enough to lure the twinkle right out of the stars in the sky, his gaze lighting with a teasing glint.

"It's easy," he said. "Like walking and chewing gum at the same time." His voice lowered an octave as he added, "I know you can handle this."

The subtle compliment held a mysterious, sexy quality that only seemed to increase the current humming around them.

"My dance steps may need a little practice—" she couldn't believe the flirtatious tone coming out of her mouth "—but I've never been called clumsy." She grinned up at him through lowered lashes. "Let's go for it."

His hand was warm against the small of her back. His shoulder felt hard against her fingertips, her other hand enveloped by his. The music could have been a physical thing, a cape or blanket that wrapped around them, seeming to cut them off from everything and everyone else in the room.

His jaw pressed against her temple, and she closed her eyes, filling her lungs with the heated scent of his enticing, bosky cologne. If there was a paradise, this was it. In Kyle's arms, their bodies close, their thighs periodically touching as they danced to the slow, soul-stirring strains, her whole emotional system seemed to shift into some kind of chaotic overdrive.

She'd grown to like the anxious and giddy feelings that rolled through her when she was with him, but having him so close—close enough to feel the corded muscles of his shoulder and chest under his jacket—made her feel light-headed and tremulous, like a blue jay that had mistakenly flown into a feline festival.

The toe of her shoe caught on the sole of his, and if his arms hadn't been wrapped around her, if he hadn't had the foresight to tighten his hold on her, she just might have stumbled to her knees.

"Sorry," she murmured, feeling terribly embarrassed.

"No need to be," he said against her ear, his voice only loud enough for her to hear.

"But I told you I couldn't be accused of being clumsy, and then I go and step right on your foot."

"Relax," he said. "You're supposed to be having a good time."

She wanted to enjoy the moment. She wanted to get lost in the feel of Kyle, in the scent of him. But she couldn't. Could it be all the lies she'd told, all the lies she'd allowed Kyle to believe, that were keeping her from having a good time? she wondered.

Her uncontrollable anxiety caused a soft, nervous chuckle to erupt from her throat, and at the same time the toe of her shoe bumped against the sole of his again.

"I'm afraid this isn't going to work," she said, humiliated to the core. "Let's go sit down."

"You just need a little practice," he told her.

Then out of the blue, he led her off the dance floor.

"Come on. Let's go." And before Cindy knew it, he'd paid the bill and they were heading for the door.

"Where're we going?" she asked as soon as she was settled into the front passenger seat of his light green sports car.

"Back to your place. If that's okay with you."

Her eyes widened in the darkness. Back to her place? Where they would be all alone? Just the two of them?

"If you'd rather not," he continued, "we could go—"

"No, no," she rushed to say. "My apartment is fine. I don't mind at all."

Mind? Why would she mind when her paradise was getting better by the moment?

He'd taken her away from the crowded restaurant and he was driving her to her apartment where they would be isolated. Alone. What should she read into this turn of events? she wondered.

The giddy feeling sprouted to life in the pit of her stomach. Were his feelings for her changing? Could their relationship really be metamorphosing into something beyond the work alliance they shared at Barrington?

"You seemed so nervous back there," he said softly.

He was speaking of the restaurant and their moments on the dance floor.

"I thought it would be better if we practiced dancing someplace more…secluded. Where strangers aren't watching."

She felt rather than saw him smile.

"That way you won't be embarrassed if you trip over your feet." There was suppressed laughter in his voice as he added, "Or mine."

The excitement inside her wilted like week-old lettuce. He didn't want to be alone with her. He was only trying to make her more comfortable on this *pretend* date they were having. The word *pretend* was more prominent in her mind now than it had been all evening. Kyle didn't want her feeling humiliated because she couldn't get the dance steps quite right.

Darn it, how had she let herself think, even for an instant, that Kyle might want to be alone with her? Disappointment rolled over her like a dark cloud. She pressed her lips together and stared out the window at the city. She felt angry with herself. It was her own fault, though. Allowing her hopes to get the better of her had been a mistake. She'd guard herself against experiencing this kind of letdown again.

"I was born and raised in Phoenix," Kyle said in the darkness of the car's interior. "My great-grandfather came to Arizona in the early 1900s looking for a job. He was one of the hundreds of men who built the Theodore Roosevelt Dam. He and his bride settled in Phoenix. So did my grandparents and my parents."

Envy tweaked at Cindy. She thought it was wonderful that Kyle's knowledge of his family tree went back four generations. Heck, she didn't even know her own father. And she'd never met her grandparents, let alone her great-grandparents. The only family she had was her mother, and she hadn't spoken to her in nearly a year.

The Silhouette Reader Service® — Here's how it works:

cepting your 2 free books and mystery gift places you under no obligation to buy anything. You may keep the books d gift and return the shipping statement marked "cancel." If you do not cancel, about a month later we'll send you 6 ditional novels and bill you just $2.90 each in the U.S., or $3.25 in Canada, plus 25¢ delivery per book and applicable es if any.* That's the complete price and — compared to the cover price of $3.50 in the U.S. and $3.99 in Canada — quite a bargain! You may cancel at any time, but if you choose to continue, every month we'll send you 6 more oks, which you may either purchase at the discount price or return to us and cancel your subscription.

rms and prices subject to change without notice. Sales tax applicable in N.Y. Canadian residents will be charged licable provincial taxes and GST.

If offer card is missing write to: Silhouette Reader Service, 3010 Walden Ave., P.O. Box 1867, Buffalo NY 14240-1867

NO POSTAGE
NECESSARY
IF MAILED
IN THE
UNITED STATES

BUSINESS REPLY MAIL
FIRST-CLASS MAIL   PERMIT NO. 717   BUFFALO, NY

POSTAGE WILL BE PAID BY ADDRESSEE

SILHOUETTE READER SERVICE
3010 WALDEN AVE
PO BOX 1867
BUFFALO NY 14240-9952

Play The *Lucky Hearts* Game

and get... FREE BOOKS, a FREE GIFT... and MUCH more!

Scratch Here!
then look below to see what
your cards get you...

Yes! I have scratched off the silver card.
Please send me my **2 FREE BOOKS**
and **FREE MYSTERY GIFT**. I understand
that I am under no obligation to purchase any
books as explained on the back of this card.

315 SDL CNGD   **215 SDL CNGC**

Name
(PLEASE PRINT)

Address   Apt.#

City   State/Prov.   Zip/Postal Code

Twenty-one gets you
2 FREE BOOKS and a
FREE MYSTERY GIFT!

Twenty gets you
2 FREE BOOKS!

Nineteen gets you
1 FREE BOOK!

TRY AGAIN!

Offer limited to one per household and not valid to current Silhouette Romance™
subscribers. All orders subject to approval.   PRINTED IN U.S.A.

DETACH AND MAIL CARD TODAY!

Kyle went on. "My parents had that sixties, New Age mentality."

The love he felt for his mother and father was extremely evident in the warmth of his tone.

"They wanted me to grow up feeling free to be me. They didn't put any kind of pressure on me at all." He glanced at her, a wide grin on his mouth. "At the ripe old age of thirty-four, I can now say that that style of parenting does have its drawbacks."

Disappointment was forgotten as she became lost in Kyle's life story. "What do you mean?"

He shrugged, leveling his gaze back onto the road ahead. "What they called freedom I now see as a lack of much-needed guidance. Kids need to talk about their options. They need some input on what to do, what to study, what to shoot for in life. As it turned out, I floundered around in college for several semesters. Having no idea what my major should be. No focus. No...goals. Oh, Mom and Dad loved me. And supported whatever decision I wanted to make. Of that I was certain. But their hands-off parenting technique was a definite obstacle for me."

Loving and supporting parents would have been a gift from heaven, Cindy thought, remembering the way her own mother had pretty much ignored her as a child. It seemed that Kyle didn't realize how very lucky he was.

"I went into business with a friend right out of college," he said. "We had quite a bit of success in Atlanta for a couple of years. Then..."

His hesitation was small, but Cindy noticed it nonetheless.

"…something happened that broke up our partnership."

He sighed, and she studied him in the darkness. She wondered what heavy burdens he was bearing, but didn't feel this was the time to ask.

"Anyway," he said, "I took a job with Barrington Corp. At the Atlanta hotel. I spent a couple of years there when a job opening in Phoenix was offered to me. Until then, I hadn't realized just how much I'd missed my home. I accepted the job, worked my way up to V.P. of New Products and I've been happy as a clam ever since."

He chuckled. The bleakness he'd expressed just a moment ago when he'd mentioned the breakup of his partnership seemed to dissolve, like a fog that had been burned off by the blazing Sonoran sun.

"Phoenix is home for me," he told her. "I'm happier here than anywhere I've been. I don't know why I wasted all that time searching for success and fulfillment anyplace else."

Kyle pulled his car into the parking lot of her apartment complex, eased into a slot and cut the engine.

His words were ringing through her mind. *Phoenix is home for me. Phoenix is home for me.*

A home. That's what Cindy was looking for more than anything else. And she was trying to make Phoenix the permanent home she was searching for. She'd lived all over the world. Felt as though she'd left tiny pieces of herself in each and every place she'd lived. Now here she was trying desperately to fill up all the empty space she felt inside her. With her beloved apartment. With her cherished friends from Barrington. With her job. Even with her wild dreams of somehow making Kyle fall in love with her.

The barren void inside her was oppressing.

Yes, she wished she'd had the kind of loving parents Kyle had grown up with. And she craved the sense of home, the sense of belonging he obviously felt for this beautiful desert city.

Cindy would never have the loving support of her mother. She knew that. But maybe, someday, she just might find a real, honest-to-goodness home here in Phoenix. Maybe. Someday.

Chapter Six

What the hell had he been thinking? Kyle wondered. To suggest that he and Cindy return to her place to practice dancing—to practice *slow* dancing—had been an idiotic idea.

He wasn't normally into self-torture. Holding her in his arms, smelling the light, flowery fragrance of her hair, her skin, was most definitely torture. To the highest degree. And the erotic music playing on the stereo was only making matters worse. Kyle knew he needed to focus his thoughts on something, anything else but the feel and delicate scent of Cindy's skin, the silky texture of her hair—

Think of something else! he commanded himself. However, he couldn't come up with a single, safe thought to latch on to.

His behavior over the past couple of weeks continued to baffle and confuse him. First, he'd kissed Cindy. His personal assistant. His employee. What on earth had possessed him? As he waltzed Cindy around her living room, where they'd pushed back the furniture to create a makeshift dance floor, he pondered the answer to that question.

The only answer he could come up with was that it wasn't all his fault. She'd completely overwhelmed him by the physical change in her appearance.

Oh, come on. A silent voice sneered at him. *What kind of excuse is that? What kind of man can't control his raging hormones?*

Okay, okay, he silently responded. So it wasn't the greatest of excuses. But *she'd* flirted with him in the conference room. She'd been the one who had fluttered those long lashes at him. Batted those gorgeous green eyes his way. So again he felt that the kissing incident hadn't been entirely his fault.

What kind of person blames his behavior on someone else?

Kyle felt he was going to go nuts if he didn't stop the questions. He also felt he was going to go nuts if he had to endure being this close to Cindy for much longer without acting on his terrific urge to kiss her. Again.

Oh, no you don't, the stern voice said. *There will be none of that. Not with Cindy. Not with* any *woman. Not after the hell you went through with Monica.*

Cindy had explained her flirtatious behavior in the conference room. And he had no reason not to believe her when she'd told him she hadn't intended to tease him, it hadn't been her aim to play with his emotions in order to get promoted to personal assistant to Mr. Barrington's son when the man finally came to take over the company. With that thought in mind, Kyle wondered why he'd continued to be so unsettled by Cindy. Before the big presentation, before her make-over and the kiss they had shared, their working relationship had been damned near perfect.

So why in the hell had he agreed to take her out for dinner and dancing? That was the worst move he could have made when his hormones were in such an uproar over the woman. And in an uproar his hormones had been. *And continued to be.* There was no denying it.

But something in him just snapped when Molly and Rachel and Cindy's other friends had talked about her dating some stranger. The idea had been very disconcerting for him. And before he'd realized it, he'd found himself offering to take Cindy out on the town.

Buff up her dating skills, indeed. Kyle guessed his *real* motive in offering to take her out was to make her realize that she should get to know a person before she trusted him enough to date him.

The mere idea of Cindy going out with this Mike from the mail room made his whole body tense with displeasure. In that moment of total preoccupation, his ears became completely deaf to the beat of the music playing on the stereo and he planted his foot, solidly and firmly, on top of Cindy's. It was her painful grimace and the stiffening of her spine that brought him back to the present.

"Sorry," he murmured. They stepped apart. "I wasn't paying attention."

"It's okay." She chuckled, lifting her knee and

reaching down to rub at her small toe. "I guess we just weren't made to dance together."

"Nonsense," he told her. "We can do this."

Kyle didn't like to fail. At anything.

"We're just finding out," he continued, "that I need just as much practice as you."

"Maybe so," she said, although a heavy doubt was in her tone. "But let's give our poor feet a break. I'll go make us some coffee."

He pressed his lips together, quelling the tremendous urge to conquer the task at hand. But rather than argue with her, he acquiesced with a small sigh. "Okay. Coffee sounds great."

His gaze automatically lowered to her slightly sashaying fanny as she left the room. Closing his eyes, he turned away, admitting that he could use a short reprieve from the battle he was waging with his overwhelming urges.

Alone in Cindy's living room, he scanned his surroundings. She had nice taste in furniture. The couch and matching chairs had big, comfortable pillows. The wide picture window was framed in a light and airy fabric that gave the room a friendly, informal feel. Just right for entertaining. Very lived-in. Homey. He liked it.

As he listened to her movements in the kitchen, he considered sitting, but then he noticed all the photos in the room. Frames of all types hung on the walls and were displayed on the tabletops. With his hands clasped behind his back, he studied the pictures that sat on the low table beneath the picture window.

He smiled at the images of Cindy as a child. She'd

been cute with her ponytails and wide green eyes. In nearly every photo, the little girl Cindy was always with a beautiful woman. Her mother, he surmised. Now Kyle knew from whom Cindy had inherited her gorgeous gem-colored eyes.

The woman with Cindy was more than attractive, actually. Her bone structure was model perfect. And in every photo she was dressed to the nines, her hair coifed just so, her nails lacquered with rich color. Yes, Kyle mused, Cindy's mother was one exquisite woman.

Frowning, he noticed something odd about the pictures. There were very few in which Cindy had been captured smiling. Usually kids loved to clown around for the camera, grinning like the proverbial Cheshire cat for the photographer. But most all of these photos portrayed a solemn, withdrawn little girl. Because the Cindy he knew was not one to be sullen about much of anything, he was left wondering what had happened during her childhood that might have made her unhappy.

Then another peculiarity struck Kyle. Most of the photographs had been cropped, a third person clipped from the image. Kyle could tell because there was usually an errant hand draped around the shoulder of Cindy's mother. A masculine hand.

Rubbing his jaw in contemplation, Kyle wondered if maybe Cindy had had some kind of disagreement with her father. Some falling-out that had impelled her to chop the man right out of her life, right out of her childhood photographs. The thought made him curious about Cindy. It also made him realize just how little he knew about the woman who worked as his personal assistant.

"I know you said you didn't feel like dessert—"

He turned at the sound of Cindy's voice.

"—but I scrounged up a few cookies. They're store-bought. I hope you don't mind. But I just don't have time to bake." She set the plate on the coffee table in front of the couch. "Coffee's perking. It'll only take a few minutes."

He nodded. "I was looking at your pictures. You weren't kidding when you said you've lived all over the world."

A tiny sigh escaped her. "I wasn't kidding."

He squelched his desire to ask her about her somber expression in the photos, and he also remained silent about the extra male hand—so obvious to him now—in most of them.

Instead he said, "Your mother's a very beautiful woman."

He seemed to sense a slight chill in the air.

"Yes," Cindy said, "she is."

Did he detect a stiffness in her tone? The obscure change in her confused him, and he wondered if he'd tread on unsettled ground. But if she had a problem with her mother, why were there so many pictures of the woman sitting around the room? Kyle decided he must be mistaken. He tried again.

"I can see now," he commented, "where you get your beautiful green eyes. Yours are the image of your mother's."

Cindy abruptly sat down on the sofa, a tiny, dubious frown planted in her brow. "You really think so?"

The vulnerability he heard in her tone had him homing in on Cindy's blatantly self-conscious expression. A realization hit him like a stone right between the eyes.

She really is unaware of just how beautiful she is, he mused.

Kyle smiled, deciding that the trait was attractive indeed. Very attractive.

"I really think so," he assured her. "I really do."

Her mouth cocked up at one corner—a tiny movement that he found utterly sexy—and she murmured a soft thank-you. However, it was clear from the tone of her voice, the lowering of her eyelids, the very set of her body, that she didn't believe a word he'd said. He wanted to reiterate, to make her understand that he was telling her the truth. She was a beautiful woman in her own right. She was attractive. Desirable. But to press the point would only make them both feel awkward.

Glancing over at the photos he'd been looking at, she said, "I just wish my mother could have been a little more interested in being a parent and a little less concerned with attracting all her *friends.*"

The bitterness coating her tone as she emphasized the final word made Kyle frown.

"We could have survived just fine without them," she continued. Then her voice unwittingly lowered to a whisper. "All I ever wanted was someone to love me. To support me."

The disclosure took Kyle aback. Her statements

were complex, and extremely revealing. So complex and revealing, in fact, that Kyle was sure he'd never grasp all of the complicated implications at which she was hinting.

Like a powerful magnet, the empty spot on the couch next to her pulled at him. He crossed the room and sat down; then he took one of her hands in his.

Knowing it was unnecessary for him to ask her to elaborate, he simply waited. She didn't disappoint him.

"I guess you could call my mother a...socialite."

He felt a small shudder course through her and he got the distinct impression that Cindy was embarrassed by the admission.

"All through my childhood, her only concern was what she looked like," Cindy said. "And who she was with."

Kyle knew she was telling him something important, something more than just the problems she'd had with her mother, but he was so disturbed by the sudden pain expressed in her clear green eyes that he couldn't make the connection.

"Moving around from place to place was an awful experience for me," she admitted. "Oh, I had everything a child could want. Clothes. Toys. Huge bedrooms all to myself. But I was so shy. So lonely. And the bedrooms would never stay the same for long before we up and moved to another city. Another big house."

Again he realized she was implying more than he was able to understand; however, he knew what she needed right now was someone who'd listen, not someone who'd ask questions.

"You see," Cindy tried to explain, "my mother was born into a family with a high social standing. She had a well-respected name. But practically no money. However, she found out quickly that she did have a commodity—her beauty. And she got by on it. Her face and body were her tickets through life."

She paused a moment, nibbling her bottom lip. "My ticket, too, I guess, since I traveled with her all through my childhood. But I decided to get off that ride. I didn't like where it took me."

When she'd told him at the restaurant that she'd grown up traveling the world, Kyle had found the idea exciting. But now he had to admit, the experience for Cindy—her *ride,* as she'd just described it—hadn't been as smooth, or as thrilling, as he'd imagined it to be.

"My childhood made me clear on one issue," she told him. "I've always been certain that I wanted to succeed on my intelligence. I wanted my ticket to be my brains, not my looks." Her chuckle held no humor as she added, "Not that I could ever get by on my *outrageous beauty.*"

The factious statement was meant to be self-deprecating; there could be no misunderstanding that. He wanted to dispute the point, but held his tongue. He didn't want to say or do anything that might urge her to stop talking about her past. He found himself feeling almost breathlessly anxious to learn more about her.

She smiled, melancholy shining in her eyes. "As a

child I used to dream about what kind of mom I'd like to have. A mom who baked cookies, who took me to the zoo, or the beach, or just for a walk in the park. I wanted a mother who would come into my classroom during elementary school to give a helping hand during parties or during art class, or who went on class trips. Other moms did. But not mine. She was too busy sunning herself. 'A woman has to keep up with her tan,' she used to say.''

Kyle got the distinct impression that Cindy's ''dream mom'' wasn't just the kind of mother she'd have liked to have, but also the kind of mother she'd like to be.

She didn't seem the least bit aware that he'd fallen quiet. She wasn't aware that their conversation had turned relatively one-sided.

Her beautiful gaze had taken on a far-off look, and he had to fight ferociously with the urge to touch her silken cheek, to somehow force those gorgeous eyes to focus on him. But he didn't dare. He never before realized that he could become so hungry for the sound of a voice—her voice—and he refused to risk doing anything that might make her grow silent.

''The most important thing I learned as a child,'' Cindy said softly, ''was the need for a person to support herself with her intelligence and her God-given talents.'' Then she nodded, almost to herself.

Without thought, she reached up with her free hand and brushed back a short, curling lock that had fallen against her forehead. At that instant he was struck with the notion that, with her guard down, with her thoughts and her conversation on the rare subject of herself, there simply wasn't a woman more beautiful than Cindy anywhere in the world. And that beauty shone from within, having nothing to do with the mascara that emphasized her long lashes or the blush softly highlighting her cheeks or the lipstick glossing her sensuous lips.

"But, you know," she continued, "something happened to me on my birthday. Something very strange. I had this…revelation of sorts."

A tiny sigh escaped her then, and Kyle feared she wouldn't continue.

"A revelation?" he prompted.

She nodded. "I'm thirty years old. I, um, enjoy my job, but the hours I spend at Barrington are just that— a job. Don't get me wrong. I do love my career. I like being self-sufficient." She blinked once, twice. "But I want a life. I want a relationship. I want someone to share with. Someone to laugh with. Someone to love. Someone who'll love me. I want children. I want a home. I want a fireplace for chilly winter evenings just like this one. I want a big, floppy-eared dog and a cuddly kitten or two."

A small crease bit into her brow as she added, "I decided that I want more. Heck, I—I want it all."

Hearing the words she'd uttered, suddenly ultra-aware of all the innermost secrets she'd revealed, Cindy's mouth clamped shut, her eyes widened a fraction and her spine went steel-rod stiff. She stood up, mindful of the awkward manner in which she'd pulled her hand from Kyle's warm and comforting embrace.

"I'm sure the coffee's ready by now."

She hurried into the kitchen and braced herself against the counter. What in the world had gotten into her? she wondered. Why would she unload all that depressing stuff about her childhood on her boss? Her *boss!* Had she completely lost her mind?

Kyle didn't care if her mother had been—and still was—a brainless debutante who flitted from man to man, who treated her only child as if she were a superfluous entity needing little or no care and attention.

"Okay, just stop," she whispered to herself in the small kitchen. If she wasn't careful, she knew the past had the potential of swallowing her up.

With shaky hands, she opened the cabinet and took down two white coffee cups and matching saucers. She concentrated on the task at hand, pulling out a tray, reaching for the sugar bowl and filling the small pitcher with cream.

She wished she didn't have to go back out there. She wished she didn't have to face Kyle. Surely she had come off looking like a whiney little brat who didn't appreciate what her mother *had* been able to provide: food, clothing, a warm place to sleep at night.

Cindy heaved a sigh, a short lock of hair flying with the effort. She needed to let him know that she did appreciate the things her mother had done for her…even if she didn't agree with the method in which the woman had gone about affording them.

The coffee smelled rich, the steam wafting in the air as she filled the cups. Then she lifted the tray, squared her shoulders and went back into the living room.

Kyle was still sitting on the couch, seemingly lost in his thoughts as he munched on a cookie.

"Here we are," she said, setting the tray down on the coffee table. She handed him a cup.

How should she start? she wondered. She couldn't just blurt out that she wasn't completely disparaging of her mother's parenting attempts. That would make her sound like a bungling idiot, and after the way she'd complained, she'd already done quite enough to lead Kyle to that conclusion. But she did want him to know that there were a few good memories swimming around up in her head.

However, before she could find a way to broach the subject, Kyle said, "Seeing as how you've come to some…ah, life decisions since your birthday, I can understand now why you're wanting to go out with this guy from the mail room, uh—" his head cocked to one side "—what was his name again?"

Cindy's heart fluttered; her whole body felt flushed as her mind went completely blank. His name. *His name.* What was the man's name?

But then she was struck with a thought. Ignoring his question, and her embarrassment at being unable to answer it, she asked, "What do you mean, you can understand now? You didn't before just this moment?"

"Well…" His tone and his expression took on a mildly defensive manner. "I just didn't like the idea that you were thinking of going out with a total stranger."

Feeling suddenly defensive herself, she said, "He's not a *total* stranger. The girls have met him."

"They've *met* him," he pointed out. "They don't *know* him."

"He's a Barrington employee," she said, not having the slightest notion about why she should want to argue with Kyle about this since it was a lie to begin with. She had no intention of going out with Mike—

Ah, yes. Mike. *That* was his name. Now she remembered. Mike from the mail room.

"It's just that," Kyle continued, "as a woman, you need to be careful. It isn't safe for you to go out with strange men."

"Strange?" Her brows lifted a fraction. "Have you heard something about Mike? Some gossip I should know?"

"Of course not. You know what I mean."

Her annoyance fading, Cindy nearly grinned at his instant and obvious discomfort. He looked so cute when he was chagrined, when his brow furrowed in that adorable way and his dark eyes gleamed with quandary. He could be so...charming. So *darned* charming. And he didn't even know it.

Suppressing a sigh, she realized that there wasn't another man on earth who could make her feel so many emotions in so short an amount of time: embarrassment, irritation, *desire*.

Every inch of her skin seemed to grow warm. He was so close to her here on the couch. So close, she could easily reach out and touch him.

"Not strange as in there's something wrong with him." Kyle went on digging himself out of the hole he'd found himself in. "I meant strange as in un-known."

She graced him with an easy smile meant to allay his self-consciousness. "I know what you meant. I was just teasing."

The attraction she felt for him at that moment was overwhelming, completely melting away her irritation like hot water poured over chips of ice.

After the slightest pause, he huskily murmured, "You've been doing that a lot lately." He set down his coffee cup and cleared his throat. "I really should be going."

"But you haven't finished your cof—"

He stood up, leaving no question of his intention to end their evening together. "I want you to know…"

Kyle paused, waiting until Cindy set down her coffee and stood up, too.

"I didn't mean to make you angry," he said. "With that comment about Mike. I really didn't."

She simply nodded, not trusting her voice enough to speak. Hearing him say goodbye was the last thing she wanted right now. Their date had gone by too quickly. At this moment it didn't matter that this tryst was pure fantasy. A pretend date. Nope, that didn't matter at all. All she wanted was to be near him for just a little while longer.

He walked toward her front door, and she followed. When he reached it, he turned to face her.

"I think we should do this again," he announced out of the blue.

"You do?"

"Mmm-hmm. You wanted to practice dating, didn't you?"

She simply stared at him.

"Well, practice means doing something a few times over," he said. "Not just once. Of course, I leave tomorrow to check out the Southern California site. But as soon as I return, we'll go out dancing again."

Cindy felt her eyes widen. She couldn't believe her luck. Kyle was going to take her out again, and she hadn't had to concoct a single lie to get him to do it. Of course, this pretend dating stuff was *all* based on a complete fabrication. But at the moment, it was pretty easy for her to disregard that fact.

"Oh," he said, "I do assume that you wanted to practice the fine art of kissing good-night."

Without giving her time to even think of a response, let alone verbalize one, he slid his hand along her jaw and leaned toward her.

"He kissed you?" Rachel sat up straight, nearly knocking over her half-empty bottle of ice tea.

"Shhh." Cindy glanced around the sparsely occupied break room self-consciously, whispering, "Do you have to be so loud?"

"But you just said Kyle *kissed* you." Her friend still sat on the edge of her blue plastic chair in Barrington's break room.

Hugging her arms around herself, Cindy groaned softly, every nuance of sheer torment she felt expressed in the ragged sound. "Yes," she said to her

friend, "he kissed me." Her tone turned utterly forlorn as she clarified, "On the cheek."

Rachel's expectant expression fell.

"Oh, Rachel, I thought I'd die. I was miserable. I
tossed and turned all night long. I was in agony, I tell
you. *Agony.* I was burning up for him. On fire."

She sighed. "I wanted to weave my fingers through
his hair. I wanted to pull his mouth to mine. I
wanted…I wanted to…" She let the rest of her risqué
fantasy fade into another sigh.

Finally Rachel said, "Well, why didn't you? It
would have been the perfect opportunity to let Kyle
know exactly how you feel about him."

"I couldn't do that!" Cindy's shoulders went stiff
with horror. "He was under the impression that our
evening together was a pretend date. *Pretend.* As in
not real. He'd even warned me beforehand that what
we were doing was *practicing* a good-night kiss."
Her facial muscles screwed up into an expression that
left no doubt about how frustrated she was feeling.
"And the whole mess is based on a wicked lie. A lie
you and my other so-called friends made up."

"A lie you went along with," Rachel softly
pointed out.

Her friend's observation made Cindy fall silent.
Then she groaned again.

"I know," she finally admitted. "I'd like to be able
to blame everyone else for this confused predicament
I'm in, but I can't. I went along with it. No, it was
more than that. I've willingly—*eagerly*—participated." Her voice dropped to a whisper as she added,
"All because I'm so darned attracted to that man."

"Stop being so hard on yourself," Rachel said. "You need to enjoy this. Every minute of it. Things might not work out how we'd like them to and all you'll have are your memories of the few dates you're going to have with him."

The perplexing half smile that suddenly tilted Rachel's lips had Cindy intrigued.

"On the other hand," her friend said, "there *is* a fine line between what's pretend and what's real. Maybe a little time together—*away* from the office— will blur that line more and more for the two of you."

Chapter Seven

Bright moonlight filtered through the filmy curtains, throwing shadows in all corners of the bedroom. Cindy tossed and turned. She was wide-awake, her body humming with need, her attempts to ignore the desire burning inside her only inflating her frustration more with each passing moment.

Sleep wasn't going to come anytime soon—that was clear to her.

Flinging back the coverlet, she swung her legs over the edge of the mattress and got out of bed. She went to the window, rubbing her hands up and down the silky sleeves of her satin pajamas.

The apartment complex supplied a play area for its residents' children, and it was the playground that Cindy's bedroom window overlooked. Of course, at two o'clock in the morning, the seesaws, swings and monkey bars were empty. Desolate and empty. Just like her life since Kyle left for California.

It had been two long days since their date. Two days since he'd bestowed on her that heart-wrenchingly sweet kiss on her cheek. Two long, empty days of working without him at Barrington.

He'd been kept so busy with site inspections that Cindy hadn't had a chance to talk to him any more than simple, quick phone calls during which she assured him the Phoenix New Products division was running smoothly in his absence.

She missed him. Terribly. Enough to cause her sleepless nights.

Never in her life had she lost sleep over a man. Never had she lain awake, tossing this way and that, unable to rest because her thoughts wouldn't stop churning, because her body wouldn't stop throbbing with hot need.

And when she *was* able to finally grab a few minutes of sleep, her mind would conjure shockingly erotic dreams. Dreams of Kyle's strong, tanned hands smoothing across her naked flesh, slowly sliding over hips, waist, breasts, his silky hair tickling the underside of her chin as his head dipped low, his tongue darting out to taste the heated nub of her nipple—

Stop! she told herself firmly. She shook her head to clear the sensuous images from her brain. She had to stop this. Or she'd never get a single moment of rest tonight.

Kyle would be returning tomorrow. Glancing at the clock, Cindy realized he'd be returning *today*. He'd be back at the office after lunch. And that meant he just might suggest taking her out to dinner tonight. Her pulse quickened with anticipation.

She couldn't wait to see him! She couldn't wait to find out how his trip went. To tell him all that had happened in the office during the two days he'd been away. He'd want to know about the erroneous figures she'd found in the report issued by the accounting department. Yes, the discrepancy was minor, but he'd still be interested. And she was anxious to hear his opinion on her newest idea. He'd probably think this current inspiration of hers bordered on being too bold, too daring for Barrington Corp. but still she...

A frown creased her brow as she stared, unseeing, into the Phoenix night. She wanted to share her thoughts and experiences with him. She wanted to listen as he told his travel adventures. She just wanted to be with him.

All this time, she'd thought what she'd felt for Kyle was attraction. A physical fascination with a very handsome man.

Yes, Kyle made her body ignite with a deep, mysterious longing, but now she was realizing that what she felt went beyond that. It went far beyond it. What she felt for Kyle was...

"Love," she whispered, a wondrous shiver coursing down the length of her spine. "I *love* him."

She couldn't believe that until now she hadn't pinned down her feelings as love. It astounded her to realize that she'd mistaken the deep emotions churning inside her as mere physical attraction.

Through all her talk about wanting a lifelong companion, children, a home—even a floppy-eared dog— Cindy knew she'd had Kyle in mind as the man of her dreams all along. So why hadn't she actually rec-

ognized her feelings as something as intense and permanent as love?

She expelled an awesome sigh. It didn't matter that
she hadn't put the correct name to what she felt. What
did matter was that she finally realized just what it
was that had her mind—and her body—in such turmoil over Kyle. And this sudden insight changed everything.

Perceiving the love she felt only upped the ante.
Knowing the depth of her feelings for Kyle made the
stakes even higher than they had been only a few
minutes ago.

Maybe Rachel had been right. Maybe she should
take a risk, do something utterly daring, something so
astonishingly forward that Kyle couldn't help but see
just how she felt about him.

Her heart hammered with fear. If she were to make
her feelings plain, he'd surely discover the big, fat lie
she'd allowed him to believe. He was certain to figure
out how she and her friends had finessed their date.
How they had manipulated him into taking her out.
Kyle wouldn't think too kindly about having his feelings exploited. In fact, he just might want to have
nothing more to do with her.

Personally *or* professionally.

Leaning her head against the glass, Cindy groaned
softly. Was she ever going to be able to escape this
utterly tangled web she'd woven?

Three hundred miles to the west, Kyle lay prone in
bed, his skin slick with sweat, his eyes open wide as
he stared into the darkness of the lonely hotel room.

The explicitly carnal dream from which he'd just awoken had his pulse throbbing, his breath heaving, his whole body rigid and aching with desperation— with a hunger so deep, he thought he'd surely starve with the wanting.

The fantasy that his imagination had concocted while he'd been innocently sleeping hadn't been the type of dream sequence with a beginning, a middle and an end, but rather, a wild explosion of isolated images that fully involved each and every perceptual sense.

Cindy's silky, brown curls had brushed his belly, causing his abdominal muscles to tense almost painfully. The mysterious woman scent of her had enveloped him like a warm, secret embrace, and even though he was wide-awake now, he thought he detected the soft flowery fragrance wafting all around him. The sight of her lithe body stretched out naked next to him had made him tremble like a weak kitten. Her creamy flesh had sent his taste buds to some titillating, ambrosial paradise. And her soft, nearly mindless moans of ecstasy, even now, made every inch of him prickle with cold perspiration as he heard the whispery memory of the sound echo through his head.

Raking his fingers through his disheveled hair, Kyle was sure his dreams of Cindy were going to drive him to the brink of sensual madness. He kicked back the sheet, his naked body still damp with sweat, and stalked across the carpet toward the bathroom door.

The tile was cool under his feet as he gazed, bleary-eyed, at his reflection in the mirror above the sink. She was like no other woman he'd ever met, his Cindy. She was talented, creative, competent...and *so damned beautiful.* He'd felt attracted to her for what seemed like forever. *Before* she'd changed her hair and makeup. *Before* she'd begun to wear those form-fitting, sexy suits to work. So why hadn't he acted on his attraction weeks—no, months—ago?

Because simply working with her had been enough for him.

He shook his head at his image in the mirror. "Why do you lie to yourself?" he grumbled out loud.

Working with the woman *hadn't* been enough. If it had, he'd have been happy to go home at quitting time, he'd have been satisfied with an eight-hour workday. However, he hadn't been happy *or* satisfied. He'd stretched out the day to ten, even twelve working hours, and he'd done what he could to make sure Cindy did the same. All because he wanted to be near her.

And the reason he hadn't acted to make his relationship with her more personal? His inability to trust. His fear of being used. A ragged sigh erupted from deep inside him.

Hell, his fear was as tall and prickly as a two-hundred-year-old saguaro. And he didn't hesitate to hide behind it.

He turned on the faucet and cupped his hands under it. Bending over, he splashed cool water into his face. Straightening his spine, he rubbed his fingers over his cheeks and jaws, droplets trailing, unheeded, down his forearms and his bare chest.

Damn it! Surely she should realize what he felt for her. Surely she should see and understand his feelings....

Why? a silent voice asked. *Why should she see what you haven't been willing to reveal? Have you told her that you think she's the most talented woman working at Barrington? No. Have you trusted her with your feelings and emotions? No. So how can she know that you want her? That your body burns for her? That you want your relationship to grow into something more personal, more intimate?*

Something more intimate... The phrase resonated through his brain, triggering a reaction in him that was both emotionally intense and physically uncomfortable.

A hoarse curse burst from him and he moved to the shower, reaching around the curtain to turn on the spray, full force and cold enough to make an involuntary shiver shoot through him. He stepped into the tub, not bothering to bite back the sharp inhalation produced by the glacial shock.

Icy water sluiced over his skin, and he closed his eyes and tipped his face upward.

No, he couldn't blame Cindy. He had only himself to blame. And now he was about to lose her. To another man she found attractive. A man who evidently didn't suffer any inability. A man who didn't hide behind any fear.

His hands clenched into tight fists. He refused to surrender! Not without a fight. Not without at least making an attempt, taking a chance, to see what he and Cindy might have together. As a couple.

Oblivious to the freezing water that cascaded over his tense body, Kyle made a decision right there and then: he wouldn't spend the rest of his life regretting what he hadn't done. He would take a risk. He would reveal to Cindy how he felt. Somehow, someway. No matter the consequences.

Cindy snapped on the small radio that sat on the console at the back of her office, and the room immediately filled with soft, slow music. She bit into the round, juicy apple she'd brought to work for her lunch. As she chewed, she sighed. The loneliness plaguing her was acute. However, the good news was that the forlornness troubling her so should be alleviated this very afternoon.

The thought was like a bright ray of sunshine burning through the dark clouds fogging her mind.

Swallowing the bite of apple, she smiled.

Kyle would be returning to Barrington today. And having every intention of greeting him as soon as he arrived, she'd decided to have her lunch right here in her office rather than eating in the break room with Rachel, Olivia and the others, as was her usual habit.

Slow, sexy notes from a saxophone smoothed over her like satin, conjuring images of the moments she'd spent in Kyle's arms on the dance floor and then again in her apartment. The feel of his arms around her like a protective cloak had been warm and wonderful.

With those sensual pictures as clear as crystal in her head, she began to sway, from side to side, right there in the space in front of her desk.

What exactly would he say to her when she saw

him? she wondered, dancing to the music. How would her greet her? With that charming, little-boy grin, she hoped. And the most intriguing question of all... Would he invite her out to dinner and dancing tonight?

He'll be too tired from his trip, an irritating voice pointed out.

Yes, he probably would be. Yet the disappointing realization didn't diminish the excitement she felt over the prospect of simply seeing the man she loved. Wrapping her arms around herself, she closed her eyes and twirled in her lovely, half-dream state. Just seeing him again would be enough.

All at once, she became vaguely aware of a fragrance hanging in the air. It causing her to frown and inhale a quick sniff. Was that the faint, yet familiar scent of Kyle's cologne? Lord, but her imagination was vivid! So vivid, in fact, that she'd nearly conjured a flesh-and-blood, three-dimentional version of him as part of this wild and wonderful lunch-break fantasy in her head, a fantasy that had her dancing in his arms.

But suddenly she was really and truly in his arms, his cheek pressed against hers as he waltzed with her for several beats. It took all of three dancing steps, three full notes of music, before she snapped back to reality, into the present. Her eyes flew open.

"K-Kyle!" she sputtered. "You're back."

"Shhh." His lips pressed close to her ear as he urged her to hush. "Just dance with me," he said.

His voice was so silky, it sent shivers coursing across her skin.

She really was in his strong, protective arms. And

the two of them really were swaying together to the sexy strains of the saxophone. All this wasn't her imagination. She sighed happily.

The music faded, and then the newscaster's mono-toned voice took its place on the radio. But still Kyle held on to her. She wondered if he meant to continue dancing, but then he pulled away from her an inch. Not too far, only enough so that he could look into her face. His arms were still holding her snugly. And that was all right by her.

His dark eyes twinkled with something not quite identifiable. His cryptic expression intrigued her. Ever so slowly he pulled her outstretched hand toward him, not taking his gaze from hers. Completely engrossed in the sensuous aura emanating from him, totally be-guiled by the curious look in his gorgeous dark eyes, Cindy let him guide her hand.

It wasn't until her fingers came into her peripheral vision that she remembered the apple she was hold-ing. Kyle pulled the piece of fruit to his lips...and with a lazy and languid deliberateness, he took a bite. Sweet, sticky juice dripped down the heel of her palm, Cindy could feel its moist path, but so mes-merized was she by his gaze that she didn't—no, she *couldn't*—pay it any mind. The atmosphere in the room constricted with something intense, and she ac-tually had to part her lips and gulp in a breath of suddenly thick oxygen through her mouth.

What's gotten into him? she wondered. Either his lunch on the plane had been so awful that he was half-starved, or—Cindy couldn't quite allow herself to believe her next thought—or *he was actually trying to seduce her.*

Her heart fluttered behind her ribs. Could he really be flirting with her?

Confusion regarding the whys and hows of his behavior made her mind spin so fast that she felt faint. Then a rush of pure panic crashed over her when she realized exactly where she was.

She and Kyle were dancing *in her office.* She was *at work.* What if some Barrington employee were to come into her office? Kyle's reputation, not to mention her own, could be badly damaged by a stirring of company gossip. Cindy felt she should step away from him, but he was holding her so tightly.

He swallowed the bite of apple, then whispered, "Have dinner with me tonight."

The overwhelming sense of joy that bombarded her brain seemed to short-circuit her thoughts. She blurted out, "To discuss your trip?"

His dark head shook, back and forth. "No. I don't want to talk about my trip. Or Days of Knights. No Barrington business tonight."

Her joy escalated to awesome excitement. "I'd love to have dinner with you."

Cindy tucked her bottom lip between her teeth, too afraid to believe that what was happening was really and truly happening. Could Rachel have been right? Could she and Kyle be crossing that fine line between what was pretend and what was real? She suppressed the hopeful sigh that hovered in her throat. Oh, how she'd prayed for that to happen.

The knock at her office door startled her right out

of Kyle's arms. She nearly tripped in her haste to step away from him, but he reached out and steadied her with a strong hand on her upper arm.

The tall man standing in her doorway had an amiable gaze.

"Cindy?"

The question in the man's tone had her smiling and nodding out of sheer courtesy.

"Patricia sent me up," he explained. "I have some papers for your department." He took a step farther into her office. "I'm Mike," he told her. "From downstairs."

Downstairs? she wondered. Ah, from the mail room, she realized. This was Mike.

This was Mike!

Until this moment, Kyle's attentive behavior had enabled Cindy to completely forget the awful lie she'd led her boss to believe. But here he was...Mike the mailman...in the flesh. And the reality of her manipulative conduct came rushing at her, blindsiding her, making her feel terribly awkward standing here with these two men.

She hadn't met Mike until now. Evidently, his delivery route didn't include New Products, and if the truth were known, she'd actually been relieved by that.

"I'm Cindy. Cindy Cooper." She instinctively switched the apple from her right hand to her left, and finding no other alternative, she gave her palm a quick swipe down her skirt before she reached out to greet him. He slid his hand eagerly into hers and gave an amiable shake.

"I've heard lots about you."

His green eyes held a mischievous glint, and in that instant she was certain that Patricia, or one of the other girls, had filled him in on the very personal situation taking place in the New Products division and his part in the peculiar predicament. Her face grew hot with embarrassment. She knew without a shadow of a doubt that Mike was "in" on the scheme they had all concocted. All she wanted to do was groan. And run to the nearest hiding place.

Not now, she silently pleaded. Why did he have to show up now?

"Mike," she said, ignoring the forward tone she'd heard in the mail carrier's voice, "this is my boss, Kyle Prentice."

She glanced at Kyle and immediately felt the need to suppress another groan. Yes, she had been able to step away from her boss before Mike had come into the room, but looking at Kyle, she wished she'd had the forethought to wipe that drip of apple juice from the corner of his sexy mouth. And here she stood holding the evidence, the darned piece of fruit. Her chagrin grew, as did the stifling awkwardness that tightened the air and crawled across her skin like dozens of tiny spiders.

"Glad to meet you, Kyle. Actually, buddy, these papers are addressed to you."

Mike's familiar tone took Cindy aback. And evidently Kyle felt the same. Her boss's dark brows furrowed.

"If the documents were for me," he said, the

words cool and curt, "then you should have delivered them to my office, rather than my assistant's."

The abrupt rebuke surprised Cindy even more, and her eyes widened. She felt embarrassed for Mike. Why, she couldn't quite say, but she didn't think he deserved a dressing-down simply because he'd delivered some papers to the wrong office.

"Kyle, maybe he did try to deliver them to you," she said, trying to ease the ever-building tension, "and he found your office empty."

She looked expectantly at Mike, sure he would latch on to this version of the sequence of events.

"No." Mike's easy grin was quite charming. "I just wanted to stop in and finally meet you, Cindy. I've heard such wonderful things about you."

It was pretty clear to her that Mike had a fun-loving attitude and didn't waste time on work-related anxiety.

Before she could respond to Mike, Kyle pointedly asked, "Don't you think you should have been focusing on delivering those papers to me? They might be important."

Mike just gave a little shrug, the smile he offered Cindy widening.

The soft groan that had been gathering in her throat finally erupted. This man didn't seem the least bit intimidated by her intense boss, and unfortunately, Mike was about to be put on report *all because of her*. It was so obvious that he was acting in this flirtatious—even brazen—manner because one of her friends had put him up to it.

"I feel the need to remind you, Mike," Kyle said,

"that you really shouldn't be conducting personal business on company time."

Cindy felt her whole body flush with panic. She had to save this poor guy. She didn't want him getting into trouble because of her. Besides, her mind silently whirled, hadn't Kyle just danced her around the room? Hadn't he just taken a seductive bite of her lunch? Was that not personal business on company time?

"There's no need to be rude, Kyle." Then she smiled at the mail-delivery man. "You'll have to excuse him, Mike. He's been away and I'm sure he's feeling tired—"

"Don't make excuses for me." Kyle's tone was sharp enough to slice off her sentence midstream.

His tone totally shocked and offended her. She simply looked at him. Then she softly said, "Well, somebody needs to make excuses for you. Or do you just enjoy acting like a jerk?"

Kyle's handsome face tightened, his hand unwittingly reaching up to harshly wipe across his mouth as if he wanted to somehow erase the few moments they had just spent alone. Without another word, he took the papers from Mike and walked out of the room.

Chapter Eight

Had she really *called her boss a jerk?*

Cindy flitted nervously around her office, straightening her desktop and console, filing papers, memos and messages, making notes for tomorrow, getting ready to leave the office for the day. Her impulsive behavior at lunch—the harsh, rash words she'd tossed at Kyle—had her terribly upset. She'd felt so scatterbrained all afternoon that she'd actually had to make a "to do" list to ensure that she completed all her work.

She hadn't seen or heard from Kyle since he'd stomped away from her office, leaving her alone with Mike.

A small smile cracked through the confusion swimming in her head. Hugging a file to her chest, she thought of Mike the mailman. He really was a nice guy.

After Kyle had left, she'd discovered—as she'd

suspected from the first—that Mike had been privy to
the lie she and her friends had concocted. And, dear
soul that he was, he'd allowed himself to be talked
into agreeing to do what he could to convince Kyle
that he was interested in Cindy.

"Oh, you were quite convincing," she'd told Mike,
the heaviness still pressing on her over how her boss
had taken his leave.

"The love of your life is awfully..." Mike had
hesitated for a split second, evidently pondering just
the right descriptive word that would accurately, yet
inoffensively characterize the vice president of Barrington's New Products division. Finally he supplied
"Intense."

She'd had to agree, but silently she'd admitted to
herself that it was Kyle's intensity that continued to
draw her, entice her. There was a power, a depth, a
profoundness in the man that she found utterly irresistible.

Cindy had told Mike that she meant to reveal the
lie she'd led Kyle to believe. She explained that she
would no longer need a conspirator, although she had
thanked him for being such a good sport about the
whole situation. Luckily Mike turned out to be an
easygoing kind of man and he hadn't been the least
put off when she'd relieved him of his "amorous"
duties toward her.

On his way out, he'd tossed a final comment over
his shoulder. "Hey, if things don't work out with this
guy and you find yourself looking for a date, keep
me in mind."

The lighthearted chuckle that had followed him out

the door had held just the right amount of breeziness to let her know he'd been teasing her. Cindy couldn't help but think that ol' Mike the mailman had better be careful, or he'd soon be discovering he'd developed a womanizing reputation, something no female would have an easy time dealing with.

Cindy sighed as she opened the drawer to the file cabinet and slid the folder into its appropriate place. The drawer closed with a click.

What she hadn't been able to figure out for the past several hours had been Kyle's blatant rudeness toward Mike. As far as she knew, Kyle had never met Mike; yet it was almost as if he had taken an instant dislike to the amiable mailman, and that wasn't like Kyle at all.

However, her boss *was* a red-blooded male. Maybe he'd felt confronted by Mike's appearance at her door. Maybe, just maybe, Kyle had felt...jealous.

Yes, a silent voice snidely commented, *and those fascinating salt banks of the Salt River would soon turn to crushed black pepper.*

Despite the negative thought, Cindy's heart raced with hope. If only Kyle's behavior toward Mike *had* been caused because he'd come to feel something for her, something wonderfully intimate. She would be the happiest woman alive.

She recalled their slow and sexy afternoon dance, remembered the lazy, almost lewd manner in which he'd stolen a bite of her apple, and her pulse pounded even faster. Could it be? Maybe...maybe...

Her chair squeaked when she eased herself down into it. She felt awful. Guilt fell across her shoulders like a lead coat. If her suspicions regarding Kyle's budding feelings for her were true… She knew full well there was a really good chance they were not— *but if they were,* then the lie she'd told Kyle now had him feeling some dark and dangerous emotions.

Mike had referred to Kyle as ''the love of her life.'' The remark had probably been made in a blasé manner, knowing what little she did about the mailman. However, she had so recently realized just how true and factual the comment really was.

She loved Kyle. Deeply. With a passion that stirred her to her very soul.

With each passing moment the love she felt for him grew, expanding and swelling, until there didn't seem to be room enough in her heart for the size and strength of her emotions.

However, this only made the lie Kyle believed about Mike all the worse.

It only made the name-calling worse, too. She hadn't just called her boss a jerk…she'd *called the man she loved* a jerk.

Her hand seemed to raise of its own volition, swiping across her troubled brow. She *had* to apologize. Not only that, but she also had to tell Kyle the truth. She was tired of living with this stupid lie.

When Cindy knocked on Kyle's partially open office door, he bid her immediate entry. She stopped short when she saw that the company president was with her boss.

''Oh.'' The tiny exclamation was out of her mouth before she could stop it. ''Kyle, I didn't know you were meeting with Mr. Barrington. I can come back later.''

"I was just leaving." Mr. Barrington's eyes twinkled with a gentle smile.

Cindy had always thought of the head of Barrington Corp. as having an almost fatherly disposition when it came to his employees. However, she also knew the man had a fierce business sense, and a fierce competitive nature, and it was this kind of professional acumen that had made this company so very successful.

"We weren't actually having a formal meeting," Mr. Barrington continued. "I just stopped down on a whim."

"Mr. Barrington would like for the three of us to get together," Kyle told her, "to talk about my trip. I told him we could see him tomorrow."

"Of course," she said, making a mental note to rearrange her and Kyle's schedules.

Mr. Barrington bid them a good evening, and Cindy found herself alone with Kyle.

She noticed that her boss was staring at the open doorway.

He was thoughtful a moment, and then commented, "You know, a lot of men in his position, after having announced their retirement, would be out on the golf course, not making it their business to continue keeping abreast of all the company happenings like he does."

"He's a good man," Cindy agreed. "A good leader. The company won't be the same without him."

Kyle asked, "While I was gone, was there an announcement regarding who will take his place?"

She shook her head. "But Mildred Van Hess did tell us yesterday that there would be news very soon. She hates company gossip and does her best to keep it at bay, but she keeps us as informed as she can without betraying confidences. Mr. Barrington will let everyone know as soon as he's sure himself."

Kyle nodded. "I'm going to be a while," he said, his thoughts evidently focused back on his own work-load. "I'm swamped with e-mails and phone messages. Some of them can wait until tomorrow. But there are a few I have to deal with now."

"I see." She took a deep breath. She'd hoped to be able to sit down and take her time telling him about her manipulative behavior. The last thing she wanted was to rush. That would only cause her to become flustered and jumble her explanation. Then the only result would be more misunderstanding and confusion between them. Finally she said, "We can talk later."

Resolving the lie might have to wait, but an apology would only take a moment. "But...if you don't mind..."

Her tentative tone attracted his full attention.

"I'd like to say I'm sorry."

He looked at her, his mahogany gaze shadowing. The ever-present tension hummed in the air.

Cindy's tone softened as she admitted, "I shouldn't have called you...that name."

She watched his jaw muscle contract and relax several times.

"You only told the truth," he finally said. "I made a fool of myself this afternoon. In front of you...and

Mike. But don't worry. I plan to apologize. He was only doing his job. He didn't deserve the dressing-down I gave him.''

The stiffness between them made her want to scream. Suddenly she blurted, ''If you want to retract your dinner invitation…''

His brow furrowed with a deep crease. ''You don't want to go?''

''Oh, it's not that at all.'' Her voice was rushed, one word tumbling over the next. ''But after what I said to you…'' Embarrassment caused her face to grow hot. ''Well, I'd understand if you changed your mind—''

''Nonsense,'' he said. He glanced at his wrist-watch. ''I'll come by your office in forty-five minutes.''

He turned away from her then, his mind obviously on more imminent business. He didn't see her vague nod. And he didn't realize that the time she would spend waiting for him would be as excruciating as if he'd asked her to sleep on a bed of finely honed nails.

Several hours later, Cindy found herself once again ensconced in Kyle's sporty car. The sigh she expelled was wistful as she sat in the dark watching the Phoenix lights grow more sparse by the moment. She didn't know where Kyle was taking her, and it didn't matter. The way she was feeling, she'd have let him drive her to the ends of the earth.

So far, the evening had been the very definition of romance. The restaurant he had taken her to had been a small, out-of-the-way place that offered them lots of seclusion, and just as much atmosphere. The table setting had been lit by soft candles. The wine had been rich and heady, and she'd probably enjoyed one glass more than she should have. The food had been delicious; however, Kyle had arrested her full attention to the point that, at this moment, she really couldn't say what she'd ordered or eaten. The music had seemed to call to them, enticing them to dance, and dance they did. She and Kyle had sauntered around and around the small dance floor. There hadn't been one misstep, not one "Pardon me for stepping on your foot" had needed to be said, they had danced together so perfectly.

And as Kyle had requested early this afternoon, their conversation had avoided the topic of work. Instead, they talked about themselves, their likes and dislikes in everything ranging from food and drink, to music and even reading material. She'd discovered he was an avid news buff, devouring the newspaper from cover to cover each morning. She unabashedly confessed that she enjoyed *watching* the news, greedily lapping up CNN and Court TV, and that her reading time was spent "escaping" from life with the latest murder mystery. Other men might have judged her harshly for this divulgence, but Kyle hadn't, and somehow, she'd known he wouldn't.

As she drove through the city, with her head fuzzy from the warm spirits and the absolutely delicious company of the man at her side, her whole body feeling relaxed, and her thoughts as well, Cindy wanted the evening to go on and on.

As if on cue, Kyle said, "I hope you don't mind, but there's someplace I'd like to take you."

"Oh." Cindy chuckled softly. "I'd love to go." *Anywhere you want,* a silent voice added.

"I was just sitting here wishing the night didn't have to end," she said.

Kyle's smile seemed to warm the dark interior of the car by several degrees.

"Me, too," was all he said.

South Mountain was the largest municipal park in the whole world. The vast mountain range had, at one time, been a Native American hunting ground. Now it served the residents and tourists of Phoenix with its miles and miles of hiking and riding trails. And although Cindy had never explored them herself, the park's steep canyons were known to reveal ancient Native American petroglyphs.

Kyle drove along the continuously elevating road to Dobbins Lookout. At twenty-three hundred feet above the desert floor, the spot offered a spectacular view of the city below.

"Oh, my," Cindy whispered, and she was out of the car before Kyle had been able to come to a complete stop.

Soon he'd cut the engine and was at her side.

"You've never been here before?"

Surprise was evident in his question.

"Only a few times," she told him. "But never at night. The view is breathtaking."

"It is."

Phoenix glowed like tiny diamonds that had been scattered across a black velvet scarf, and Cindy had

the thought that she could stare at the dazzling pan-
oramic scene for hours and hours without becoming
the least bit bored.

An involuntary shiver shook through her, and Kyle
noticed.

"Come here," he said. He stepped behind her,
pulling her back against his chest, wrapping his arms
around her and clasping his hands intimately beneath
her breasts. The temperature in the city's center had
been at least ten degrees warmer than it was up here
on the mountain. Kyle made a warm coat and she
didn't hesitate to snuggle back against his hard, yet
yielding body.

Cindy didn't understand exactly what was happening between them, couldn't fathom what it was that
had caused this change in Kyle, in their relationship.
However, she wasn't plagued by any anxiety to discover the reasons behind his sudden gentle and loving
treatment of her. She only knew she liked it.

The lie, a guilty voice whispered across her brain.
*Tell him about the lie. Set him straight so whatever
is happening between the two of you won't be totally
ruined.*

The spectacular view of the city was blocked out
when she slowly lowered her eyelids. This wasn't the
first time tonight that she'd been censured by the re-
proachful voice inside her. But so far, Cindy hadn't
been able to find the correct opening line, or the right
time to bring up the awful subject.

"I have something I want to tell you."

Cindy was startled by Kyle's words. They were the
exact ones she'd been about to utter herself.

Curiosity got the best of her, and she let her need to confess her sins slide away to the back of her mind as she wondered what it was he wanted to say. But even her interest in his impending disclosure wasn't enough to contain the overwhelming happiness that swelled inside her chest.

Isn't this what she'd longed for all along? A relationship with Kyle in which they could freely talk to one another? A closer, more personal connection in which he felt able to reveal his private thoughts and feelings with her?

Yes! she thought. This was exactly what she'd been looking for. This was really a dream come true.

"I haven't," Kyle began, softly whispering the words against her ear, but his words quickly petered out. After a short moment, he tried again. "I haven't always been as...trusting and open with you as I'd have liked."

He sighed, his breath blowing the strands of her hair and tickling the sensitive skin behind her ear. But Cindy stood stock-still, sensing that what he was about to say was going to be immensely significant to her. To them both.

"But there's a reason for that," he continued. "A reason that I'd like to explain to you."

Gently reclining her head back against his shoulder, she looked up into his face. "I'd like to hear." She knew her gaze conveyed the deep sincerity she felt in her heart. "I'd very much like to hear."

And then, thinking that the telling would be easier for him if she wasn't staring him in the face, she raised her head and fixed her gaze on the sparkling city down below.

Kyle's second sigh wasn't quite as deep, nor as formidable as the first. She guessed he was still feeling distressed about what he wanted to say, but Cindy felt her encouraging assurance regarding her interest had helped to alleviate some of his anxiety.

"The story starts out quite a few years ago," he said. "Right after college, I got together with a buddy of mine. We started an advertising agency. We were partners, Don and I, as well as best friends, and we were successful at what we did.

"We used to hang out at a busy diner. We'd have lunch at Jude's Place. And with our late hours we'd often have dinner there, too."

His voice tightened as he said, "Monica worked at the diner. Doing the accounting. She was…smart. And pretty. We became a couple, she and I. I talked Don into hiring her at our agency. And for months, things worked out just great. My relationship with Monica seemed on the fast track, if you know what I mean. We moved into an apartment. Lived together for nearly a year."

Cindy felt his throat convulse with a swallow, and she used his pause to take a deep inhalation, not realizing until that moment that she'd been breathing so shallowly. She hadn't wanted to miss a word he said.

"Monica was hungry to learn the business inside and out," he continued. "And I was happy to teach her everything she wanted to know. She started bringing in clients. She was a real asset. So when she asked me to make her a partner, I didn't hesitate."

He shrugged. "Hell, I was happy to. I'd thought we were in love. I'd thought we were headed for a future together. Marriage. Kids. A house in the suburbs. The whole bit."

Again he sighed, this one evincing a deep and distinct sadness. He whispered, "I was so wrong. I lost my head over that woman. And my heart."

Quite a few moments passed in total silence. The mountain air was chilly, but Cindy was warm enough with Kyle's arms firmly about her shoulders.

"It wasn't until I asked her to marry me that I caught on that something was wrong," he said. "She just stared at me in total disbelief. Then she turned me down. Flat out declined my offer, she did. She asked me why I wanted to go and mess up our perfect arrangement, 'our mutually beneficial arrangement.' That's exactly what she called what we had together, what we'd been living."

His body seemed to stiffen behind her, as though his memories made him grow cold.

"It was then," he went on, "that I realized I'd been taken for a ride. Lied to. Used. Manipulated. Monica didn't love me. She had never loved me. She'd only wanted what I could provide her—an exciting and successful career in a successful business. And she'd been willing to sleep with me to get it. She'd even been willing to continue sleeping with me to keep it. I was sick. Just sick."

Absently he unclasped his hands, slipping one inside the facings of her coat and settling it on her tummy, shifting the other so that he could curl his fingers into her palm. It was so obvious to Cindy that he needed some support, and she gave him what she could, gently and empathetically squeezing his fingers with hers.

"By this time Monica had wiggled her way into every aspect of the firm. She was an important part of the company. Don had come to rely on her keen business sense as much as I had. So I stepped out of the picture."

Remembering what he'd told her in her apartment about leaving his business, she asked, "That's when you came to work for Barrington Corp.?"

She felt him nod. "I've been working for Mr. Barrington ever since."

Cindy felt impelled to ask, "What happened to the ad agency?"

"As far as I know," he told her, "they're still going strong." As an afterthought, he added, "Don and Monica still send me a Christmas card every year."

Releasing her, and gently planting his hands on her hips, he turned her around to face him. They looked at one another for several long silent moments.

"I don't know what to say," she finally breathed. "It's awful. What Monica did to you."

Unwittingly, he moistened his bottom lip with his tongue. "What's awful is that I allowed myself to become very protective of my heart. Of my emotions. I couldn't trust anybody with what I was feeling. I couldn't even trust myself. I was too afraid of being lied to. Of being used."

His chest expanded with a slow, steadying inhalation. "But I think I'm ready now. I think I'd like to…to try."

His dark eyes were full of questions, full of hope, full of fear. Cindy wondered if the fear she saw was

over how she might react to his story. Or if the emotion there was fear that she might reject him. She
wasn't totally sure, but she knew how easy it would
be to assuage his apprehension.

Reaching up, she slid her hand along his cheek until his jaw was tenderly cupped in her palm.

"I'm glad you told me."

He closed his eyes, tilting his head a fraction toward her hand, and suddenly Cindy felt overwrought
as a myriad of emotions churned inside her. Her gaze
splintered with moisture. She simply didn't believe
that, in her whole life, she'd experienced a happier
moment than this one, right here, right now.

His story tumbled around in her brain. Monica had
been a wicked person, a vicious, self-centered woman
who had hurt Kyle terribly. No wonder he hadn't
wanted to become involved with anyone else. No
wonder he'd been afraid to trust. And no wonder he'd
reacted so adversely when she'd tested him about taking the job as the assistant to Barrington's new president.

*I'd been lied to. Used. Manipulated. Lied to...
used...manipulated.*

His words echoed in her head, like a mantra that
had been shouted from atop the vast canyons of South
Mountain.

Cindy realized that she, too, had lied to Kyle. She'd
used him. Manipulated him. All for her own gain.

Just like Monica.

Like muddy water solidified to crystals of dirty ice,
her insides froze.

Oh, Lord, Cindy silently prayed, *how can I make*

him understand? How can I ever make things right between us?

Kyle was reaching out to her, confiding in her, telling her his deepest secrets. And how would she repay him? By telling him that she was as bad as the woman in his past—the woman who had caused him such pain and anguish.

He hadn't actually told Cindy that he loved her, but he'd come awfully close. He'd said he wanted to trust. He wanted to try. She was on the brink of actually seeing the realization of her dreams. Only to watch them tumble over into a huge precipice of hopelessness—all because of her own foolish behavior.

Finally Kyle opened his eyes and gazed into her face. "I can't tell you how good this is for me. I've wanted to tell you for so long. How I feel about you, I mean."

He pulled her against him and she tried not to stiffen; instead she splayed both her palms on his chest, staring self-consciously at the backs of her hands.

His fingers, strong and warm, slid under her chin and tipped up her face until she was forced to look into his eyes.

"I'm so glad you know now. So glad."

His voice grated over her ears, across her skin, hot and sensuous. And then without giving her a moment to move, to think, to respond, his mouth descended to hers.

Chapter Nine

His kiss was hotter than hot, his tongue blazing across her lips like the molten desert sun. Cindy had no other choice but to surrender to the searing heat and she melted against his hard chest.

Pressed to him tightly, her nipples contracted into tiny buds so tight that she nearly gasped, her breasts aching with the need to be touched. A sudden rush of sizzling desire coursed through her veins, turning her blood thick and fiery as lava, leaving her utterly breathless.

And while her emotions walloped her from the inside, Kyle continued his assault from without. His fingers threading through her hair, his tongue wreaking havoc on her mouth, the feel of his rigid manhood pressing firmly against her hip.

A small sound escaped from the back of her throat and she parted her lips, bidding him entry—an offer he didn't hesitate to accept.

He tasted faintly of warm wine, but he was much more intoxicating to her senses than any inebriant could ever be. Her brain fogged, her thoughts simply ceased to be and her equilibrium felt terribly unbalanced; the whole world seemed to shift off-kilter. In a desperate effort to regain some kind of control, she gathered the fabric of his shirtfront in her hands, holding on for dear life.

Parting the facings of her lightweight coat, he slid his arms around her body, his hands gliding up her back feeling toasty warm compared to the mountain chill. All that stood between them was the thin fabric of her blouse, the mere idea of him being so close making her exhale softly against his mouth. Unwittingly she arched her spine, pressing herself into him even closer. She heard his breath catch in his throat, and then he groaned, a sound so rich, so sexy, so *riveting,* that she was shaken to the very core by the earthquakelike tremble that shuddered through her.

The thought that *she* had caused the moan that had erupted from deep in his chest, that *she* was the reason his breath had hitched, sent her into a passionate frenzy. Reaching up, she wove her fingers into his dark, silky hair and she deepened their kiss further. Their tongues danced to that silent and slow, erotic and ancient rhythm.

Danced.

And danced.

Finally Cindy could stand it no longer. She wanted to feel his hands on her bare skin, wanted to see him naked, wanted to touch every part of him that was now covered with clothing.

"Come on." She tugged at his shirt, his jacket, her voice filled with ragged frustration. "Let's go back to my apartment. I...I *need* you."

"Oh, honey..." His voice, too, came out as a grating whisper. "I need you, too."

"Then come on," she urged him. "Let's go."

He spent a few long, sensuous moments nibbling at her neck, her jaw, her ear. Cindy closed her eyes, luxuriating in the feel of his hungry lips on her skin. However, if he didn't touch her—*all of her*—soon, she knew she'd surely shrivel up and die right there where she stood.

Ever so slowly, Kyle skimmed his hands over her body, from her back, around her waist, and then he settled them so that his thumbs just grazed the sensitive undersides of her breasts. Time seemed to stand still, her breathing stopped, as she waited for his next move.

Her grip on his shirtfront relaxed, and she flattened her palm against his heart. The pounding she felt there was like the trampling hooves of a hundred horses, and the feel of it simply thrilled her.

"Please," she said, not the least embarrassed by the desperate whimper she heard in her tone, "can we go?"

Again he groaned, burying his face in her jaw-length curls and hugging her to him.

Kyle hadn't used the word *love* tonight, but whatever emotions he was feeling for her had prompted him to kiss her, to touch her, in an extremely intimate fashion. Was she shortchanging herself by willingly offering him everything she had to give—her mind, her body, her soul—before she was really certain—

She terminated the thought completely. She was more than happy to simply ride this wave of passion and not try to figure it all out just now. There would be plenty of time later for pondering and conjecture. At this moment, the hunger pumping through her—*through them both*—took precedence over everything.

"Honey, I think we *should* go," he finally said.

Eagerness and a heavy anticipation colored her tone when she answered, "Good."

But when she made a move to go to the car, he held fast to her. A deep frown planted itself in her brow as she looked into his face.

Starlight glittered in his sexy dark eyes; however, the ebony night hid from her whatever it was he was feeling, thinking. But one thing was clear: his hesitance.

"What is it?" she whispered.

He took what seemed to be a deep, soul-stealing breath.

Finally he softly repeated, "We should go. Back to your apartment." He paused long enough to swallow before adding, "But I won't be coming in."

In that instant, Cindy discovered what true deprivation was. She felt like a starving person who was denied even a few crumbs of food. No, she felt worse. She felt like a starving person who had been about to sink her teeth into some succulent and tender morsel, only to have it cruelly wrenched from her hands.

She trembled. "But why? I don't understand. I—I

thought you…'' The words faded into ''Don't you want—''

Reaching up, he gingerly pressed his warm fingertips against her mouth. ''Hush,'' he said. ''Listen to me.''

She closed her eyes, wanting desperately to purse her lips and gently, lovingly kiss the pads of his fingers, but the disappointment swirling inside her kept her from doing so.

''I *do* want,'' he assured her. ''The wanting in me is so strong it hurts.''

Cindy's gaze softened. *Let me ease the pain,* she tried to relay with a look. *Let me fulfill your need.*

She knew full well that the silent offer was the most selfish she'd ever made in her life. Satisfying his need would be no sacrifice for her, for doing so would be the only way she'd satiate her own.

His jaw tensed, and he looked away from her for a moment, clearly communicating that he understood her soundless missive.

Finally his dark eyes were once again riveted to hers.

''We have to take this slowly,'' he said. His voice dropped to a husky whisper that was barely audible as he added, ''*I* have to.''

They stood there studying one another in the cool mountain night. Then she took the only option open to her: she yielded to his wish with a reluctant sigh.

The days that followed were the most wonderful of Cindy's life—*as well as the most miserable.*

She and Kyle had been kept extra busy at work

now that plans for Days of Knights had been approved by Mr. Barrington. And their evenings were spent sampling the most romantic nightlife Phoenix had to offer. They had visited cozy restaurants—one that featured live jazz performers, another that offered a blues band, and still another whose specialty was twanging country music. Kyle had taken her to the ballet at the Herberger Theater Center, and they also enjoyed a lovely concert at the Phoenix Symphony Hall. She was discovering that the city had a huge amount of cultural entertainment to offer.

As she rode the elevator down to the ground floor, Cindy actually smiled when she remembered their conversation last night.

In passing, Kyle had mentioned to her that he intended to purchase tickets to the Arizona Opera Company. She hadn't missed the reluctance he'd tried to hide, so she had quickly told him she'd much rather go to see the Phoenix Suns play at the America West Arena. He'd been relieved, obviously and overwhelmingly so.

"Are you sure you want to go see a basketball game?" he'd asked.

Heck, she'd thought, basketball wasn't the most romantic way to spend an evening or the most culturally fulfilling, but she could tell by the excited twinkle in Kyle's eye that he'd very much appreciated her suggestion. And, surprisingly, making him happy gave her more pleasure that she'd ever imagined it would.

"Oh, I'm sure," she'd told him. "To tell you the truth, operatic drama really isn't my thing."

He'd shaken his head and smiled. "Mine, either,"

he admitted. "If I'm to be perfectly honest, I hadn't tried very hard to buy the opera tickets."

The guilt expressed on his handsome face could have been equated to a little boy who was confessing that he'd stolen cookies from the cookie jar. Cindy had found it so charming, so endearing, that she couldn't help but chuckle at him. Thankfully he hadn't been offended but had joined in with her laughter.

Each day—and night—that they spent together served to bring their relationship closer.

Why, then, she wondered, had she not told him about the awful lie she'd concocted with her friends? Why had she not been forthcoming with her manipulative behavior where Mike the Barrington mailman was concerned?

She stepped off the elevator into the building's high-ceilinged foyer and then walked down the hall on the way to the break room to fill her coffee mug.

The reason she kept the secret hidden was all Kyle's fault. Whenever she'd been about to tell him, he'd unwittingly take her hand, or gaze into her eyes, or stroke her hair, and immediately all thoughts of revealing the lie dissolved, there and then. In fact, whenever his attention was focused on her, Cindy actually had trouble formulating thoughts and words. The man just had that mesmerizing effect on her, that was all there was to it.

His touches, his caresses, his hot and passionate kisses at the end of every evening, were the very things that had made her life so very wonderful. On the other hand, the ongoing lie, like a stubborn, thorn-ridden vine that absolutely refused to die, had been what had made her life so utterly miserable.

A sigh escaped from her lips. She knew it wasn't fair of her to blame Kyle for her dishonesty. Charging him—or rather, charging his stunningly romantic behavior toward her—was too easy. And she wasn't in the habit of taking the easy way out of anything.

There was no use trying to fool herself. She was the one who was at fault. She simply didn't have the guts to tell him what she and her friends had done. Not when she knew that by doing so she'd destroy every bit of the intimacy that they had worked so hard to build—not to mention the trust.

It had taken him years to bring himself to express to someone the pain and anguish that Monica's manipulation had caused him, and Cindy had been so happy that she had been the person he'd confided in. Kyle was now working on getting over it; he was slowly moving beyond the emotional distress that that woman had caused him. And it was his inner pain that was keeping Cindy and Kyle's relationship from developing to that most intimate, physical plane. To tell him that she, too, had plotted and planned against him, finessed and exploited him…

She shook her head. The news would only obliterate the trust he was slowly beginning to place in her. He'd be devastated. He would never forgive her; she knew that without a shadow of a doubt.

The thoughts weighed heavy on her mind as she pushed open the door to the break room.

Normally she'd have gotten caught up in the hustle and bustle of greeting her co-workers. A few people were clustered here and there at the tables, some enjoying an early lunch, others just taking a short coffee break. Cindy had so much to do today that she didn't intend to linger, she meant to pour herself a cup of coffee and then make her way back up to her office. However, she did allow her gaze to sweep over the room. If her girlfriends were there, she wanted to be sure to take the time to say hello.

Well, she didn't see Rachel or Sophia or the others, but she did see Kyle. He was standing next to the large coffee urn talking to Stanley Whitcomb, one of Barrington Corp.'s lawyers who worked with Cindy's friend Olivia in the legal department.

Her steps slowed. Whatever the two men were talking about, the subject had Kyle puffed up like a veritable peacock. And Stanley looked to be thoroughly enjoying her boss's remarks.

The closer she got to the two men, the more intriguing their private conversation—and Kyle's body language—became to her.

Cindy was forced to stop a few feet away from Kyle when someone reached out and touched her sleeve in greeting. She spent half a minute exchanging pleasantries with the table of people. Unwittingly, she became aware that she was able to overhear what her boss was saying, and she was stunned to discover that *she* was the topic of the one-sided discussion.

"Stan, she's just so damned beautiful," Kyle said.

Evidently he didn't realize he was being overheard by some of the people in the room. Or maybe he did and he just didn't care.

"When I walk into a restaurant with Cindy on my

arm,'' he continued, ''every male eye in the room turns to stare. I'm tellin' you, it's a great feeling. Knowing other men are envious of me makes me fly high as a kite on a windy day.''

Cindy's insides froze into a solid block of ice. In that instant, she was transported back to her childhood. The utter loneliness she'd felt all those years ago filled every nook and cranny inside her. Then a terrible confusion fought for space in her crowded mind—confusion over why her beautiful mother would neglect her only daughter, why she would give all those suitors priority over her little girl. And then fear crashed over her like a giant, life-threatening wave. Fear of all those faceless, nameless men who loved being with her mother, but who hadn't cared one whit about the ''tagalong'' child. Anxiety of starting at yet another school, learning her way around yet another city or town, settling in at yet another huge and lonely mansion, estate or château, the awful feeling of knowing you had no friends to speak of and wouldn't have until you could force yourself out of your isolating shell of shyness and apprehension.

Emotions battled within Cindy; all the while she heard echoed memories of the litany of compliments her mother invariably received from her many lovers.

I feel like such a man with you by my side... absolutely invincible!

Your beauty alone is well worth any trouble I must go through in order to have you.

My dreams are haunted by your lovely emerald eyes.

The compliments were spread, thick and smooth

and sweet as creamy butter on bread. And there's nothing that would twist a child's idea of loving relationships more than to be forced to listen to such empty words of flattery being bestowed onto the one person she looked to for nurturing.

Anger boiled up in her chest—hot, acidic and bitter. She could no more stop it than she could thwart a bolt of lightning or halt thunder from rumbling across the stormy desert sky.

Trembling from head to toe, she closed the distance between herself and Kyle. Even the startled expression in her boss's gaze when he finally saw her wasn't enough to knock her out of her angry state. Her stern, unsmiling face seemed to confuse him, but she couldn't concern herself with that. She set her empty coffee mug on the counter and didn't give it another thought.

"I do want you to know—" She kept her voice low enough not to be overheard by anyone but Kyle and Stanley. It wasn't her intent to make a scene, but she had to let both these men know exactly how she felt. "—that I take great offense at being discussed over the company water cooler."

The white-hot fury evinced in her statement evidently shocked Kyle even more than her sudden appearance had, for his dark eyes went wide, his spine straightened and the frown creasing his forehead bit even deeper into his brow.

"I am *not*," she continued, "a piece of meat to be displayed in the butcher's window. No matter how much pleasure that might give you."

Her anger grew more heated by the moment. Cindy

knew she had to get out of the room or risk being the brunt of the office gossip for weeks to come. So without saying another word she turned around and marched herself across the room and out the door.

Kyle stood just outside Cindy's office door, staring down at the empty coffee mug he'd carried up with him from the break room. He wouldn't be able to figure out women even if he was to live as old as Methuselah.

Cindy's anger had blindsided him but good. He'd never have guessed that his braggadocio words to Stan would stir her ire to the point that she'd actually turn into a small but deadly tornado.

He shook his head, one corner of his mouth curling up. She'd been a little fireball, she had. Cute as could be with her anger all stirred up and blazing. He was sure that he could explain what he'd said, that he could make everything okay. It wasn't like he'd meant to offend her. The pride he felt over simply having Cindy in his life had just gotten the best of him, that was all. And that pride had spilled out during a conversation with Stan. Surely he could make Cindy realize that.

No, he'd never understand the opposite sex.... His grin widened. But he was sure having a damned good time trying.

Kyle knocked and then pushed open the door.

Cindy was standing behind her desk.

Bypassing a greeting altogether, he said, "We need to talk."

She didn't stop flipping through the papers she was sorting.

"I said everything that was on my mind," she told him. "I think it would be best if we just steered clear of one another for a while."

He still thought her anger was cute, but her request took him aback. "A while? What do you mean 'for a while'?"

"Oh, a day or two. A week. Maybe a lifetime."

She went to the file cabinet, jerked on the drawer handle, stuffed in a paper, then slammed shut the drawer.

Maybe a lifetime?

This wasn't so cute anymore, he mused. What the hell had he done that was so wrong?

"Cindy," he began, "I obviously made you angry—"

"You figured that out, did you?"

"Whoa," he said softly, trying hard to contain a situation that seemed bent on spiraling completely out of control. "Wait just a minute."

She stopped midway between her desk and the file cabinet, her arms crossed tightly over her chest, her mouth a firm, straight line. Everything about her, even the air around her, felt closed off, out of reach. She simply stood there, staring at him.

Finally his own anger was stirred by the frustration he felt at not being able to soothe away her irritation.

"What did I say that was so awful?" he asked. Without waiting for an answer, he barreled ahead, full steam. "If it's an apology you're looking for, well then you're out of luck. I refuse to ask forgiveness for simply speaking my mind to a friend. I would think that any woman would feel good about being bragged about by the man in her life.''

But the logic seemed completely lost on her.

''Kyle, I spent my whole life around men who did nothing but boast,'' she said. ''They strutted and swaggered around. All the while my mother simpered and cooed and batted her big, gorgeous eyes. It was disgusting. My mother was involved in at least a dozen so-called 'loving relationships.' And I want nothing to do with anything even remotely resembling them.''

Before he could respond, she continued. ''I want to spend my life with a man who loves me for who I am in here—''

She poked at her chest, just above her heart.

''And for who I am in here—''

This time she poked at her temple.

''My mother used her beautiful eyes and her curvy legs and her...her perfect boobs to get...*things*. My mother and I survived on her looks.''

The grief in her green eyes made him want to take a small step backward, but he held his ground.

''But I don't have to do that,'' she said. ''I've got brains. I've got an education. I've got enough business sense so that I can survive without simpering and cooing.''

At that moment, Kyle remembered all the photos in Cindy's home, all the cropped pictures. Then the vague reference she'd made regarding her mother's *friends* came back to him. Cindy had said that she wanted to be noticed for her intelligence. His mind churned. Why hadn't he understood before? Finally the puzzle pieces started falling into place.

"Honey, no one is asking you to simper and coo." He tilted his head a fraction. "You're preaching to the choir here. I work with you. I know you're intelligent. I know all about your terrific business sense. I see it every single day."

But what he said evidently fell on deaf ears.

"I don't want my life to be filled with empty relationships," she repeated in a rush. "I won't be my mother. I won't live her life. Going from man to man...just to...to survive."

Cindy's disdain for her mother suddenly got under Kyle's skin.

"What makes you think your mother enjoyed how she lived?" he asked. "I don't know your mom. I don't know what kind of person she was. Or is. All I know is that I can't imagine anyone enjoying the idea of living off other people."

"*Men,*" Cindy stressed. "My mother lives off wealthy men."

Once she grew silent, Kyle softly said, "Okay, wealthy men. I just can't believe that's something that she wants to do. Have you ever tried looking at her motivation? Have you ever tried to figure out why she'd *choose* to live her life the way she does?"

"It's something she's always done. How she's always gotten by."

Kyle heard a note of defensiveness in Cindy's tone, and it clearly told him that she hadn't never tried to see the situation from her mother's point of view.

"But why?" He spoke the question as tenderly as

he could. Remembering what little she told him of her mom, he said, "Maybe she felt she had no other choice." Then on a whim, he blurted out, "Maybe she did it for you."

"Me? What are you talking about? I had nothing to do with it. Nothing!"

"Can you be sure? Have you ever asked her?"

"No, I've never asked her. And I never will. Those kinds of questions would only embarrass us both."

"Or they could bring you back together."

She only glared at him, resentment glittering in her eyes. The feelings inside her regarding her childhood were intense, and they ran deep; he could clearly see that.

Kyle understood in that moment that it wasn't him or his boastful remarks she was angry with—it was her mother, and the residual bitterness she felt over the manner in which she'd been brought up.

"You told me," he said, "that your mother had a good family name, but no money. Maybe she found herself with a daughter to raise and no means with which to do it. Maybe she made her way the only way she knew how—"

"She could have gotten a job!"

"Maybe she had no skills. Maybe she had no self-confidence. Maybe she—"

"Stop, Kyle! Just stop this right now."

Cindy's face, her whole body, became rigid with agitation.

He shook his head, determined to help her even though she thought she didn't want his help. "Your mother was adamant that you got yourself an education. You told me that yourself."

"She sent me to college," Cindy said, "because she said I wasn't pretty enough to survive on my looks."

Quietly he pointed out another possibility. "Maybe it was because she didn't want you to have to."

"I'm not listening to any more of this." Her voice was on the verge of being described as a shout. "How in the world did we start talking about my mother, anyway? This argument has nothing to do with her."

The tears he saw gathering in her green eyes just about broke his heart in two. He wanted so badly to make her see, to force her to understand that their quarrel had *everything* to do with her mother. Everything.

"I'm angry because I heard you bantering about a bunch of meaningless trite about me. And I won't have it. I won't!"

With that firm declaration made, she rushed from the room, leaving him all alone in her big, empty office.

Chapter Ten

"What in the world makes him think he can treat me that way?"

When Cindy stormed out of Barrington's New Products division, she hadn't a clue where she was going and had been surprised when she'd found herself pushing through the glass doors of the legal department. Thank goodness the documents she'd inadvertently carried from her office needed to be sent to the legal staff anyway. Cindy guessed the papers had been on her mind and she'd subconsciously continued to work, even though she was fuming about Kyle, and that's why she'd ended up unloading all her frustration on poor Olivia.

Her friend had taken one look at her when she'd arrived, and had shoved her into the nearest conference room where they could talk without being overheard. Cindy then spent the next ten minutes practically chewing off Olivia's ear with almost everything that had been said between herself and Kyle.

"I mean," Cindy continued, "he was talking about me like I was some kind of trophy or something."

"You said that already," Olivia quietly pointed out.

It was the first time her friend had spoken since they went into the conference room and the sound of someone's voice other than her own made Cindy grow still.

Realizing suddenly how upset she'd been, how she'd ranted and raved, Cindy murmured, "I'm sorry. I shouldn't be burdening you with all of this."

"It's okay," Olivia assured her. "I'm your friend. I want you to come to me."

"Yes, but I shouldn't act like I'm—"

"It's okay." Olivia stressed her words with a gentle touch on Cindy's forearm.

The warmth of another human being, one who cared about her as much as Olivia obviously did, melted away some of Cindy's anger. Her emotions felt like the sails of a huge sloop on a windless day— the massive fabric was still there, but they were no longer stretched taut and billowing. Cindy suddenly felt weary and she rubbed her fingertips across her forehead.

"Listen to me," Olivia said.

The reservation in her friend's voice wasn't lost on Cindy. She was about to be told something she probably wouldn't want to hear. Cindy lifted her chin to look Olivia in the eye.

"I'm not so sure that Kyle did anything so terrible."

"What?" Cindy's gaze widened with disbelief. "How can you say that? Didn't you hear me say he talked about me like I was a piece of prime rib? Didn't you hear me when I explained why I couldn't allow myself to be treated that way?"

"I did." Olivia kept her tone calm. "And I do understand why your childhood memories are bad ones for you. But you can't lump Kyle and his comments in the same barrel with the men you grew up around. Because there's a distinct difference."

Cindy's raised brows were a silent request for her friend to continue.

"You said it yourself," Olivia said. "Those men your mother was with didn't mean anything they said. And you knew that because your mother never stayed with any one of them for long. Even as a child, you were astute enough to come to the conclusion that those compliments were empty. But like I said, *there's a difference with Kyle.*"

Her friend's caring gaze grew even more serious.

"Kyle cares." Olivia pressed her lips together, tucking back a strand of her long auburn hair as she evidently waited for Cindy to respond.

"How can I know that?" Desperation and frustration welled up inside Cindy. "How can any woman know that a man is being sincere?"

After a moment, Olivia shrugged. "No woman can know it. She's got to feel it."

Cindy grew so weak in the knees that she eased

herself down into one of the large padded chairs surrounding the big rectangular table. Olivia immediately pulled out a chair, sat down next to her and took
her hand.

"Do you have any idea," Olivia continued, "how
much I'd love to hear...to hear a man talk about me
the way Kyle was talking about you?"

Stanley Whitcomb, Olivia's boss, was on her
friend's mind, Cindy was sure.

Olivia continued. "Me and Molly. Rachel. Sophia.
Patricia. Every single one of us want to be exactly
where you are. We want to have the man we love
extolling our virtues. Crowing about how they feel
about us."

Had that been what Kyle had been doing? Cindy
wondered. Had she been too sensitive about his brag-
ging remarks? Had she blown his comments out of
proportion?

Her childhood memories had crowded in on her,
had made her react first and think later. Much later.

Olivia was right. No woman could ever truly know
if her man was being honest and sincere. But the same
went for men, didn't it?

Kyle wasn't at all like the men in her mother's life.
Cindy knew it. *She felt it.* She always had. That's why
she'd been drawn to him from the first.

And what about her mother's life-style? Could it
be possible that Kyle had been right? That her mother
had lived the way she did—not because she liked it—
but because she knew no other way to survive?

Could Kyle also have been right about why her

mother had urged her to get herself educated? So she could be independent and self-reliant?

One thing was certain, Kyle had made her rethink her opinions regarding her mother. She'd always been so bitter and close-minded about her past. Maybe she should give her mother a call...open up the lines of communication. Who knew what might come of it?

The more Cindy mulled everything over, the more she saw just how different Kyle was from any other man she'd ever met. He'd touched her life in ways no one else had, not even her girlfriends here at Barrington. Yes, Kyle had made an awesome impact in her life. He was different, yet she and he had something very much in common.

With what he'd gone through in his past, Kyle was just as distrusting of the opposite sex as she. Even more so. Cindy had known that for a while now. But that knowledge hadn't kept her from responding so angrily when she'd overheard Kyle talking about her. Slipping her bottom lip between her teeth, she realized that her deep love for him caused her to act irrationally. Time and again.

Feeling her eyes tearing, Cindy whispered, "Olivia, I love him so very much."

"I know you do. Maybe now's the time to tell him."

Cindy's exhalation was full of self-disgust. "I can't tell him now. I've ruined everything."

Olivia squeezed her fingers in commiseration. "Maybe you haven't."

Lowering her eyelids, Cindy groaned. "Even if

blowing up at him in the break room in front of Stanley wasn't bad enough," she said, "there's still the matter of that stupid lie I told him about Mike."

"*We* told him," Olivia reminded her.

Cindy only sighed. In an effort to be discreet, she had held back the information regarding Kyle's past experience with that awful woman named Monica, so Olivia wouldn't understand that sharing the blame would never soften the blow when Cindy's manipulative behavior was finally revealed.

Evidently trying to bolster her friend's spirits, Olivia said, "Besides, you said that when Kyle was talking about you to Stanley, that his voice was full of pride. Maybe he hasn't said he loves you, but his feelings for you must run deep."

Despite her solemn mood, a humorous grin broke out on Cindy's mouth. "I think the words I used were 'his voice was full of cockiness.'"

Olivia chuckled softly. "Pride. Cockiness. When it comes to a man's emotions, don't they mean just about the same thing?"

They shared a poignant smile.

Then all at once, Olivia's face seemed to turn a sickly shade of green. She closed her eyes and placed the flat of her hand on her stomach.

"You're still sick," Cindy observed.

Olivia only nodded. "I'm okay. It'll pass quickly. It always does."

"You need to see the doctor. This bug has gone on for far too long."

Cindy had suspected for a couple of weeks now

that this "bug" her friend suffered from wasn't the flu at all. That it was something much more life altering. But she couldn't force Olivia to confide in her. She could only be there if the need to talk ever arose in her friend as it had for her today.

"I'll go see my doctor," Olivia said.

"Soon?"

Her friend gave her a nod of promise.

"But right now," Olivia said, "you need to go find Kyle. Talk to him. Spill your guts. Tell him exactly how you feel."

Cindy shook her head miserably. "Talking won't help."

Tugging on her arm, Olivia pulled her toward the door. "Talking *always* helps."

"Not this time," was all Cindy said.

The elevator door whooshed open and Cindy stepped out onto the fourth floor. She needed a few minutes to think. To plan. Her office would offer a quiet haven in which to gather her thoughts before she approached Kyle with everything she had to tell him. She only hoped she could get to her office and shut the door quietly without running into Kyle in the hallway.

When she slipped past his office, she was pleased to see his door was shut. Turning the knob of her own office door, she pushed it open, feeling immensely relieved that she'd have some time to contemplate just how she'd—

"You're back."

The sound of Kyle's voice made her nearly jump out of her skin. Evidently he saw that he'd startled her.

"I'm sorry," he said. "I didn't mean to frighten you."

Cindy made a valiant effort to recover. "I—I'm okay," she stammered. "I just didn't expect to see you. Here. In my office."

Kyle obviously couldn't stop the soft chuckle that slipped through his sexy lips.

"That *is* where we are," he observed lightly. "In your office."

After a moment of awkward silence, Cindy said, "I, um, I took some papers to Legal. I, um, didn't expect to see you. Here."

Darn it, she was repeating herself. This awful anxiety she was feeling had her thoughts and her tongue all tied up in knots. Again he chuckled, a sensuous sound that only tightened the coils of her already-tense nerves.

But he quickly subdued his humor. "I know you didn't," he told her. "But you left so abruptly before. I thought I'd hang around so we could talk when you got back. I thought if I explained a few things to you, you might feel a bit differently about what happened in the break room." He paused a moment, then asked, "Do you have time? To talk, I mean?"

His deep chocolate eyes darted around the room and then lit on her face. His shoulders were rigid, his fingers slowly curled and then straightened, curled and then straightened. Cindy realized at that moment that Kyle was apparently just as uptight as she. What in the world did he have to be upset about? she wondered.

She really couldn't concern herself with whatever it was that had him feeling disturbed. She needed to focus on all the things she needed to tell him. Once she was finally free of the lie, she'd feel better. Her relationship with Kyle would most likely be ruined beyond repair, but at least her mind would no long be encumbered with the gray shadows of guilt.

"I do need to talk to you," she told him. Then she steeled herself with an huge inhalation. "I have some things I need to tell you. Some things I should have told you long ago."

"Me, too," he said. "I have some things I need to tell you. Things I should have told you long ago."

The fact that he repeated her words, verbatim, took her aback.

"*Long ago...?*" Her brows furrowed, her own admissions fading to the back of her mind. "B-but what things should you have said...?"

He came to her and took her by the arm. Cindy allowed herself to be led, so flabbergasted was she by what he'd said. He guided her to her desk, then turned her around and gave her a gentle push so she'd relax her rear against the rounded oak edge.

Kyle moistened his lips, paced away from her the length of two steps, then he paced back. He looked momentarily distracted, like he was mentally rehearsing his lines. Cindy had the fleeting thought that she wished she'd had that luxury.

Finally his handsome chin tilted up, his gaze focused on her, extremely intense, making her feel like she was the only living being on the earth.

"I want to tell you," he slowly began, "that I think you're a beautiful woman."

The profound quality she heard in his declaration made her feel terribly self-conscious, and she fought back the panic that gathered in her chest.

"Well," she quipped, "with fifty bucks' worth of makeup and a monthly trip to the hair salon, you, too, can be a beautiful woman."

Kyle didn't laugh. He didn't even smile. And the fact that her joke took a complete and utter nosedive only inflated the thick awkwardness that threatened to drown her.

He sighed, his dark eyes seeming to tinge with what looked like sadness.

"The beauty I see," he said, "has nothing to do with makeup and hairstyles."

The fact that she'd made light of him had hurt him; that was clear and she murmured an apology.

"What I want you to know," he continued, "is that I've been...attracted to you for some time."

Cindy's cheeks warmed. She knew that ever since she'd coerced him into taking her out on that first date that their attraction for one another had blossomed like a snowy white cactus flower in spring.

Then he added, "Longer than you imagine, I'm sure."

If he was going to continue to surprise her like this, she was going to have to sit down. She was desperate to ask him what he meant, but the plea for him to elaborate simply refused to form on her tongue. Luckily he didn't wait for her appeal.

"Long before your birthday," he continued. "Long before your friends took you out for a—a complete…"

"Overhaul?" she supplied, her voice a mere whisper. His words so astounded her that she was amazed that she'd been able to come up with a description of the birthday present her friends gave her.

The tiny crease in his brow disturbed her, and she wanted to reach out and smooth her fingertip across it. But she didn't. She was too afraid to act. Too afraid she'd make another wrong move. Too afraid that she was in the middle of some wonderful dream and she didn't want to wake up.

"I'm going to say it again," he told her. "You're a beautiful woman. On the outside. But especially on the inside."

He reached up and caressed a lock of her hair. "It wouldn't matter if every single one of these glorious curls fell out. It wouldn't matter if you were to wear a burlap sack. I'm still going to love you."

Cindy couldn't stop the grin that split her mouth. "A burlap sack. I doubt Mr. Barrington would approve of—"

The realization of what he'd actually said hacked off her words like a razor-sharp saber. He was so close to her that she could smell the wonderful scent of his cologne, but still he seemed much too far away.

"You're still going to…?"

"Love you," he softly provided.

As if he knew his declaration was a shock to her, he reached out and placed steadying hands on her shoulders.

"I've cared for you for months and months," he said. "But my fear, my distrust, kept me from acting on my feelings. And then you came into work looking absolutely ravishing."

His mouth curled into a sexy half grin and his eyes clouded over, almost as if he was reliving the memory in his head.

"Yes, you showed up at that meeting looking like a goddess," he continued. "More beautiful than words can describe." His gaze focused on her once again as he added, "And I was lost."

He gave a small sigh. "But I was in deep trouble. How could I tell you how I was feeling…how I *had been* feeling about you? I couldn't. Not without looking like some kind of lecherous Casanova. Not without looking as if your makeover made all the difference."

The look on his face seemed to beg for her understanding. "The change in your appearance didn't cause my feelings for you. But your makeover *did* force me to act."

Kyle gave her an ironic smile. "When your friends told me you were interested in going out with Mike, I nearly panicked. I was saved when they asked me to take you on that pretend date." He chuckled. "I don't know if you noticed back then, but I've never agreed to anything so fast in my life. I saw the opportunity as my only chance to somehow show you how much I cared for you.'' His tone softened. ''And then after spending so much time with you, I realized that I not only care for you very much, I love you with every ounce of my being.''

Cindy's heart twisted painfully in her chest. She should be happy. She should be ecstatic. This fiercely intense man had just confessed his love for her. She should be filled with overwhelming joy.

So why wasn't she?

Because she had some confessing of her own to do. There was a secret that needed to be revealed. A secret that would surely destroy everything.

Confusion lit his brown eyes, his brow wrinkling with obvious worry.

''You don't seem happy about what I've said.''

When she finally found her voice she said, ''Oh, but I...I...''

She let the sentence go unspoken. She wanted so badly to lean against him. To kiss his mouth. To let him know in no uncertain terms just how deeply she loved him. Just how joyous she felt to hear him verbalize his emotions. But she couldn't. Not until she told him everything. Every last ugly truth.

''I have some things I need to tell you,'' she said, averting her gaze from his. ''Some things that aren't going to be very pleasant for me to say. But I'm going to say them because they need to be said.''

For the span of two heartbeats—and two heartbeats only—Cindy considered not telling him about the lie at all. What would it hurt? Her friends would never divulge the secret. Not if she asked for their confidence. And not telling him would surely save him— it would save them both—a great deal of anguish and heartache.

But it wouldn't be right. Even if she didn't love him, the immense respect she felt for him was enough all by itself to have her confessing the truth. A friendship couldn't be based on lies, half-truths and manipulations. She'd tell him. *Because she loved him so very much.*

After a moment, she emphatically murmured, "They simply *must* be said."

He tipped up her chin with his crooked index finger and gazed into her eyes.

"You seem afraid," he observed.

"I am," she told him. "I'm very afraid."

The love and concern expressed in his gaze nearly stole away her breath.

"Honey, there's nothing you can say that will change how I feel about you."

She bit her lip, fighting back the tears that prickled the backs of her eyelids. "You'd better not say that," she warned. "Not until you've heard me out."

After a long, soul-searching moment, he said, "I'm listening."

She closed her eyes, swallowing nervously. Hurting him was going to be awful. But disappointing him would be worse. His trust was about to be betrayed. And she was the betrayer. There was no getting around it. There was no softening the blow.

Her thoughts churned frantically, latching on to the perfect means of putting off the inevitable.

"First," she said, her voice a grating whisper, "I want to thank you."

Kyle's curiosity creased his already-worried brow even further.

"I've spent my whole life thinking that my mother liked living the way she does. And I've resented it bitterly. And that bitterness has colored my views of loving relationships. It never dawned on me that my mother may feel trapped and unhappy."

Absently Cindy reached up and smoothed her bangs out of her eyes. "You made me see that there might be another explanation." She gave a small shrug. "And that alone is enough of an incentive for me to reach out to her. To talk to her about my feelings. To offer her the chance to talk about hers."

She touched his warm hand with the very tips of her fingers. "I want you to be the first to know. I'm going to call my mom. And no matter what our conversation brings, I'm going to tell her that I love her. Because I do love her. No matter what may have happened in the past. I think she did the best for me that she could." Her head tilted, her gaze softening. "And I only have you to thank for that. You made me stop. You made me think."

"I'm glad to hear you're going to call your mother," he said.

But his whole body was stiff and waiting. And she knew she could put off the bad news no longer.

Suddenly her chest was filled with a terrible sadness, a sadness as vast and desolate as the Sonoran Desert. Hot tears welled up and spilled slowly down her cheeks.

"Oh, Kyle," she said around the hot lump of regret that had formed in her throat. "I'm so sorry you fell in love with me."

She got the distinct feeling that she couldn't have shocked him more even if she'd smacked him across the face.

"I don't deserve your love. And when you find out what I've done, I'm afraid you won't even *like* me anymore, let alone love me."

His grip on her grew suddenly desperate. "Honey, you're killing me. Please tell me what this is about. What is this horrible thing you think you've done?"

She tried to look away—she didn't want to see the hurt and pain her confession was about to cause him—but he cradled her jaw in his palm, forcing her gaze to lift to his.

Her tears felt like liquid fire as they scalded their way down her face.

"I lied to you," she whispered. "I manipulated you. I'm no better than that woman from your past. Monica. And just as she didn't deserve the love you have to give, neither do I."

Cindy became aware of how quiet the room was, and Kyle grew utterly still as he awaited further explanation.

"The whole idea of my going out with Mike, the guy from the mail room, was a farce," she said, her voice unsteady with soft sobs. "It was a lie. A lie I concocted to make you jealous. A lie that led you to offer to take me out under false pretenses. I never dreamed that that one night would lead to so many others.'' She paused, sighed. ''That's not true,'' she amended. ''That's exactly what I'd dreamed would happen. But I feel just awful that I was dishonest. I feel terrible knowing that this beautiful relationship that has grown between us has ugly roots. Roots tangled with lies and manipulation.''

She felt like she couldn't catch her breath, like she was drowning in her own misery.

''All I can say is—'' she took an instant to drag oxygen into her lungs ''—I'm sorry. I fully understand your aversion of being manipulated and lied to, and I'll also fully understand if you never want to see me—''

The sound that erupted from Kyle cut her words to the quick. Her heart pinched when she first heard what she thought was a groan of sheer agony. But then her eyes flew open wide when she realized that Kyle was laughing. *He was laughing.*

Confusion turned her thoughts to chaos. Had her admission hurt him so much that he'd lost his senses?

The next thing she knew, he was kissing her soundly on the mouth.

It wasn't a long kiss, or terribly romantic, but it was enough to send Cindy's head swimming. She'd never been kissed by someone whose laughter made it difficult for him to pucker.

What is going on? she couldn't help wondering.

"You went to those lengths just to make me jealous?"

His dark eyes twinkled gaily.

She gave a mute nod. She didn't understand. Why wasn't he angry? Why wasn't he insulted? Why didn't he take offense at her deceptive, conniving behavior?

"I don't understand," she began, but he chuckled again and she grew still.

"Honey," he said, his voice gentle, "how can you possibly compare what you've done to what Monica did? It's not the same at all. Not at all."

She truly felt foggy with bewilderment.

"The difference," he continued, "is all in the motivation. Monica's incentive for manipulation was completely selfish."

"B-but so was mine." The words sounded weak and far-off to Cindy's ears.

He shook his head. "No. Not really. Monica cared only for herself. She cared only for her career. She didn't care about me at all." His fingers smoothed over her tearstained cheek and his tone lowered as he commented, "I get the feeling from what you've told me, though, that you *do* care."

She leaned against his touch. "More than I can ever express," she whispered. "I love you, Kyle."

"And I love you."

He kissed her then, a kiss that was soft and warm and full of promise.

Suddenly he smiled against her mouth, and the

thought fighting to get out was what evidently made him pull back.

"Although, if I remember correctly, it was Molly and Rachel and Olivia and the rest of your friends who told me about Mike. They were the ones who suggested I take you out on that first pretend date. They're the ones who conjured the lie."

Her heart swelled with remorse. "But I went along with it. And I went on allowing you to believe it. And for that I'm very sor—"

He stopped her with another feathery kiss.

"All I can say is thank you," he said. "If you hadn't forced me into action...if you hadn't pushed me into taking you out and facing my past, we may never have gotten together." His dark gaze glittered. "I intend to thank all your friends, as well." He shrugged good-naturedly. "Heck, and Mike, too."

At last Cindy was able to smile. She reached up and pulled him into her arms.

He whispered against her ear, "How soon will you marry me?"

She gasped and leaned back to look at him. "What did you say?"

He studied her for a long, languorous moment and then quietly said, "I asked you if you'd become my wife."

"Oh, my." The tears that blurred her vision and spilled down her cheeks were filled with a joy the likes of which Cindy had never known. Her birthday wish was coming true. Suddenly every single empty space inside her seemed filled with warm, wonderful emotion. She felt whole. Finally.

I'm marrying my boss. The mere thought was enough to have her floating among the clouds.

"Well?" he asked, obviously impatient for her answer.

"Oh" was all she could murmur. She was going to have to do something to cope with the wonderful chaos the man of her dreams caused her thoughts to fall into.

Since she couldn't get her tongue to form an affirmative response, she planted on his lips a heated kiss that was sure to convey her answer perfectly.

Yes!

*   *   *   *   *

Don't miss Olivia's story,

THE NIGHT BEFORE BABY
by Karen Rose Smith,

next month's LOVING THE BOSS title,
available only in Silhouette Romance.

This March Silhouette is proud to present

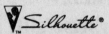

SENSATIONAL

MAGGIE SHAYNE
BARBARA BOSWELL
SUSAN MALLERY
MARIE FERRARELLA

This is a special collection of four complete novels for one low price, featuring a novel from each line: Silhouette Intimate Moments, Silhouette Desire, Silhouette Special Edition and Silhouette Romance.

Available at your favorite retail outlet.

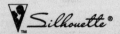

If you enjoyed what you just read,
then we've got an offer you can't resist!

Take 2 bestselling
love stories FREE!
Plus get a FREE surprise gift!

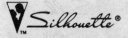

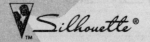

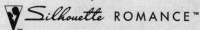

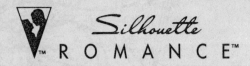

Silhouette ROMANCE™

COMING NEXT MONTH

#1348 THE NIGHT BEFORE BABY—Karen Rose Smith
Loving the Boss
The rumors were true! Single gal Olivia McGovern was pregnant, and dashing Lucas Hunter was the father-to-be. So the honorable lawyer offered to marry Olivia for the baby's sake. But time spent in Olivia's loving arms had her boss looking for more than just "honor" from his wedded wife!

#1349 A VOW, A RING, A BABY SWING—Teresa Southwick
Bundles of Joy
Pregnant and alone, Rosie Marchetti had just been stood up at the altar. So family friend Steve Schafer stepped up the aisle and married her. And although Steve thought he wasn't good enough for the shy beauty, she was out to convince him that this family was meant to be....

#1350 BABY IN HER ARMS—Judy Christenberry
Lucky Charm Sisters
Josh McKinney had found his infant girl. Now he had to find a baby expert—quick! So he convinced charming Maggie O'Connor to take care of little Ginny. But the more time Josh spent with his temporary family, the more he wanted to make Maggie his real wife....

#1351 NEVER TOO LATE FOR LOVE—Marie Ferrarella
Like Mother, Like Daughter
CEO Bruce Reed thought his life was full—until he met the flirtatious Margo McCloud at his son's wedding. Her sultry voice permeated his dreams, and he wondered if his son had the right idea about marriage. But could he convince Margo that it wasn't too late for their love?

#1352 MR. RIGHT NEXT DOOR—Arlene James
He's My Hero
Morgan Holt was everything Denise Jenkins thought a hero should be—smart, sexy, intelligent—and he had swooped to her rescue by pretending to be her beloved. But if Morgan was busy saving Denise, who was going to save Morgan's heart from *her* once their romance turned real?

#1353 A FAMILY FOR THE SHERIFF—Elyssa Henry
Family Matters
Fall for a sheriff? Never! Maria Lightner had been hurt by doing that once before. But when lawman Joe Roberts strolled into her life, Maria took another look. And even though her head said he was wrong, her heart was telling her something altogether different....